"Now I realize h[...]
anyone who will op[...]
it ... People who know how to love are
able to conquer anything they desire."

Also by Ernest K. Gann
Published by Ballantine Books:

BAND OF BROTHERS

A HOSTAGE TO FORTUNE

THE AVIATOR

ERNEST K. GANN

BALLANTINE BOOKS • NEW YORK

Library of Congress Card Number: 80-68543

ISBN 0-345-30405-5

This edition published by arrangement with Arbor House Publishing Company

Manufactured in the United States of America

First Ballantine Books Edition: February 1982
Second Printing: April 1982

For my friends and comrades who pioneered the world aloft. For those who survived . . . fair winds. For the many who were lost . . . fair winds.

Preface

1928 . . . like 1914 was a last year of innocence for much of the world. Only a very few foresaw the catastrophic financial events which began in North America the following year and soon affected all nations. Then innocence died once more, as it had when the cannons were silenced in 1918. It seemed that once each decade or so what was loosely dubbed "society" must endure a violent transformation.

In 1928 the overwhelming majority of young Americans believed fervently in God, honor, duty, and country. They were proud of themselves and usually of their life work. This was particularly true of airmen, many of whom first ventured aloft during the Great War that ended in 1918. They were often men of dash and predilection for hazard. They were instinctively obliged to continue in a profession which was opening new frontiers almost daily. Practicing it was still an art. It paid them modestly in money, but lavishly in broken bones and death.

They formed their own mold, the Lindberghs, the Slonigers, the Roscoe Turners, and the Joe Smiths. Many of their kind died with their boots on while flying the mails.

The survivors passed on their hard-won knowledge to younger pilots who became the "Captains" of the future and replaced artfulness with science.

Air-mail pilots were not considered as solid citizens, but as bad insurance risks. Most did not really care because they were enamored of flight. They lost themselves in it as a man may sometimes utterly abandon himself to an enchanting woman. Their words did not limp when they spoke of flight although shyness was peculiarly common among them. Enthralled in their flying life, they were innocent of most worldly things.

The vehicles which bore these men through the lower altitudes were fragile creations of elementary design. Given enough power and they would fly, although their engines were temperamental and sometimes betrayed their trust. Navigational aids were non-existent along many air-mail routes and the airmen wound their way in good weather and bad by employing a combination of experience, daring, and cunning. They found in themselves a sort of sixth sense of chance and direction because they had to, and as a consequence many developed the fierce independence known to old sailors and desert Touaregs.

This loyalty to and reliance upon self was true among airmen of all countries, although the more technically advanced British and Europeans did enjoy primitive radio communication with earthlings. Except in the eastern United States, American airmen did not and thus, once launched into the sky, they simply disappeared. After a certain amount of time they reappeared—without ceremony and without anyone on earth aware of their interim whereabouts.

Sometimes they did not reappear. . . .

1928

Now the pilot glanced down at the terrain and knew again a momentary sense of foreboding. Unless the weather was very fine it was always the same through here. The mountain plateau was high and devoid of human trespass. Here the surface of the earth seemed to be made of roughly cast iron. Bold and barren escarpments served the pilots who flew this way as recognizable markers in a rumpled ocean of rock and desert. It was wild country and there had been times when the pilot wondered if it were possible to fear land itself.

He glanced down at the grey scud which was unquestionably congealing into a solid overcast. There were still breaks here and there; the mouths of pits torn in the vapor revealed grey rock teeth and scrubby black trees at the bottom of the throats. Tendrils of soupy cloud hung from the peaks which towered in the distance, but they did not immediately concern the pilot. He was preoccupied with studying the overcast above him. It could squash him.

Before he had taken off from Elko in Nevada and headed north the pilot suspected the weather might be deteriorating. And he supposed it might not be the best of days. But then, he was flying the mails and was not expected to squat on the ground like a frightened canary every time there was a cloud in the sky. If a pilot showed an obvious preference for flying only in the best conditions he soon found himself looking for work. This was the way of his life and he had always ascended even when others had found excuse to keep their feet on the ground.

He listened for a moment to the steady thunder of the Wright Whirlwind engine which gave his aircraft flight. He thought of it as a beautiful engine and he was glad he was not sitting behind a Liberty—one of those leftovers from the war which had lasted long enough for him to learn to fly and finally qualify as an instructor. He smiled. Now, still courtesy of the same generous government, he was air-borne, swimming like a tiny sperm cell in an enormous womb. Because he had spent much of the past ten years aloft he had come to accept the fact that here he was almost at home if not quite. To be totally at home in the air, he knew, a man must cease being mortal. Even so, he thought, here is the only place I am content.

Although the route was prescribed, every flight was different. There was the weather according to the seasons which in this region of the North American continent presented violent contrasts. The environment of each flight also differed because of the time of day or the wind. Usually it blew from the west but the velocity was capricious. During strong winds the flight became a wrestling match as he worked to keep the Stearman bi-plane on a reasonably straight and level course. It was a good airplane, fashioned of the finest woods, the best wire, and the stoutest fabric. While it was smaller than the old De Havillands and Pitcairns flown in the same service across the eastern states, it was stronger, more maneuverable, and less likely to ailments. More importantly the Wright engine was not cursed with the plumbing problems which afflicted the De Havilland's Liberty.

The pilot thought there was no more dependable aircraft engine in the world than the nine-cylinder

Wright Whirlwind. He knew its heavy drumming would now be echoing over the plateau below and he was easy about trusting his life to it. Thus far my one and only life, he mused. Too dumb to be a lawyer . . . too lazy to be a doctor, too restless to become a merchant. Who directed one man to achieve fortune and stability while another became a gypsy? Many men ended their one life at this work—abruptly. Those who fancied they were unkillable often proved their faith had been misplaced.

It was the way of things aloft. There were certain things an aviator might attempt even though they were inherently dangerous, but good chance and foolishness were not at all alike.

This flight was different from most because he had a passenger. She was a little blonde girl and he had decided she must be about eleven or twelve. A guess, of course, but then he knew so little of such matters. Or was she a hundred and one?

Her parents had brought her to the airfield at Elko and they had said her name was Heather.

The pilot had declared it was a pretty name and her answer had come instantaneously. "It has rosy flowers and in Scotland sometimes they make brooms out of it." Her eyes sparkled as if she were challenging him and he found her smile disconcerting.

"Out of what?"

"Heather—"

"Sure . . . of course." His mind was on the shortness of the days at this time of the year, for if the weather turned foul, slipping into Pasco at night could become sticky.

When he had asked her parents why they were sending her to Pasco by airplane rather than by rail Heather had not given them a chance to reply. "My grandfather has this disease and ever since he can't see very well. So my parents thought I would have much more to tell him about if I saw like a bird."

The father shrugged his shoulders and the pilot thought he must have been long dominated by his family. The mother only smiled.

"Have you ever flown before?" he asked the girl.

"No. But sometimes I act it out . . . like if I was a real bird."

"Good for you. If you're a good girl on the flight this morning maybe I can teach you to see like a real bird."

"I don't like to make promises that are tied to something. It's a sneaky way of getting people to behave differently from what they really are."

The pilot was not sure why he had suddenly become so uneasy. It was hard for a bachelor to understand children, and he thought that if they were brash and bright it was even more difficult. And then, any passenger was a nuisance. Considering the look of the weather he would certainly have preferred an adult.

The take-off was already more than an hour late because Probosky the mechanic had said he would feel better if he changed several plugs on the Whirlwind engine. Finally, when he was done and the pilot was heaving the mail sacks up to Probosky, who stowed them in the bin, the girl tapped his arm and asked, "When do I get my parachute?"

"You don't." He heard the annoyance in his voice and regretted it.

"Why not? Don't you have a parachute?"

"Yes. I'll be sitting on it. My seat was designed to fit around it and it's sort of a cushion. You ride up here in the mail bin right on top of the sacks so you'll have plenty of cushions."

"Well, I want a parachute. Supposing I have to jump out?"

"Do you get everything you want?" Now he wondered why he had been compelled to taunt her. Even if she was spoiled rotten it was not his obligation to reform little girls at ten o'clock in the morning. She would be just a body in the mail bin ahead of him for a few hours and then he would never have anything to do with her again. Let be, let be, he thought. At thirty-one, was he becoming crotchety?

"At school my English teacher Miss Atcheson told me I would have a parachute so I know I'm supposed to have one."

"Miss Atcheson is wrong. We don't furnish parachutes to passengers because for one thing jumping out of an airplane is a very dangerous business and you have to know exactly what you're doing. I've never jumped out of an airplane and I'm not going to today."

"You better not."

The girl was pouting and he decided what she really needed was a spanking. And yet . . . and yet there was something very special about her.

Now the time was nearly noon and he saw the sun appear momentarily through a break in the overcast and he thought how often he had witnessed the same development. Standing at the zenith the sun would be viewed through the most shallow part of a flat overcast. Seen obliquely it must dim or be gone entirely. Or was it, he thought, as his passenger turned to glance at him, just being shy?

He would have liked to share his questioning with the little girl, but rendered aloud by a man of his age, he thought, it might sound silly. And Heather did not seem in the *least* silly.

Against the cold he knew they would encounter he had borrowed a flying suit like his own, a great "teddy bear," as the garment was known to the profession. Heather's parents and everyone around the Stearman had laughed hilariously while they tried to fit her into the teddy bear.

"We need six more of you to fill it up," the pilot had said. "Heather, you won't even fill a leg."

"My name isn't Heather."

"Oh? Then what is it now?"

"Dorothy. And I'm on the way to see the Wizard."

Finally he carried her to the Stearman because she could not walk in the teddy bear. Perhaps it was the way she clung to him with her arms around his neck and her blue-green eyes looking up at him that made him wonder at her magic. And perhaps his present fascination with her had meant more than he realized. How long had he starved for the touch of another . . .

Now, remembering the delicious sense of holding such a lovely little creature even for a moment . . . He warned himself that such recollection was dangerous. It could lead to the self-pity he had long managed to avoid. It could lead to other memories.

He reached forward into the slip-stream and tapped the girl gently on top of the leather helmet he had loaned her. As was customary when carrying the occasional passenger, the metal cover of the mail bin had been removed. She resembled, it occurred to him, a little sparrow, perched on the sacks.

She turned quickly to look back at him and he hoped he had not alarmed her. He held up his gloved hand and made the questioning sign with his fingers for "okay?"

She smiled and nodded vigorously. The helmet was too large for her and he saw how the slip-stream lifted it from her forehead and teased a brush of her blonde hair. He thought the thin band of freckles across her nose only added to her beauty and he was pleased to see her eyes so full of excitement.

He formed the words "Are you cold?" with his lips and he shivered to illustrate his question. She shook her head and laughed although he could not hear her above the roar of the slip-stream. At one hundred and twenty miles an hour it was like trying to carry on a conversation in a hurricane.

It *was* cold. It was always cold in these mountains in December and he supposed the temperature at this altitude was below the twenty degrees indicated by the new little dial on his instrument panel. Why did he mistrust it? Because it was new? Was he becoming set in his ways like so many of the older pilots—like old sailors always opposed to change?

He did trust the other instruments arrayed before him. There was a gauge to show his speed through the air and the needle was now quivering slightly as if to prove its alertness. The Kollsman altimeter announced he was holding the aircraft steady at eight thousand feet. There was a rate-of-climb instrument with a needle hovering a hair below horizontal. An indication of constant descent. The instrument was lying, provoked by his personal habit of trimming the Stearman slightly nose-heavy and thus gaining a minute advantage in cruising speed.

There was a turn-and-bank instrument, consisting of a ball free to roam like a bubble in a carpenter's level and a pointer known as "the needle." A magnetic compass just under the windscreen gave him direction. There was also a clock which in this Stearman did not function. The hands stood at ten past four.

There were also instruments to tell him of the health of his engine. They announced the oil pressure, temperature, and revolutions per minute.

These were the simple tools of his craft. Combined with the flight controls, a stick projecting between his knees for maneuvering about the vertical and horizontal axis and two rudder pedals to control the lateral axis, he was able to pilot his aircraft to any destination within range of its fuel.

Like any experienced workman he had come to trust his tools, but most of all he trusted himself.

The girl turned to look back at him. He saw her eyes questioning and her lips form the words, "Where are we?"

He throttled back the engine momentarily and shouted, "You're still over Nevada. It will be another hour before we are over Idaho!"

She smiled and looked down. Then she looked back

at him and he saw her smile fade. Her eyes were still questioning, but her lips did not move, and after an instant she turned her head away.

Angrily, he shoved the throttle full forward and some of his desolation was lost in the snarl of the engine. Why had he been so busy convincing himself that for some unique reason she seemed to be different? Why had she been so long in seeing what everyone else saw?

Instinctively he touched his glove to the side of his face he knew would never go away. And for an instant his yearning for physical tenderness nearly overwhelmed him. The right side held a bare hint of the handsome youth he had been in photos of eight years past, but the left? Beginning just below the scalp line was an ugly mass of tortured scar tissue, pitted and ravined and accented by a slackness in the lower left corner of his mouth. It was the best job the doctors could do to a face that had first been smashed to a bloody pulp and then scorched by exploding gasoline. By some miracle the left eye had emerged unscathed, but no surgical miracle could replace what had been lost in the crash on that long-ago terrible morning.

There were hard-noses who said that an instructor who lost a student when he was sitting right with him in the airplane would be better off dead.

Soon after the removal of the bandages he had learned to present the right side of his face to the world. The other side made people squirm and it was even worse when they were overpolite.

When this sort of thing happened the pilot found it convenient to think of Moravia—because alone among most men Moravia understood. Moravia had flown in the Great War to save the world for democracy and he had also been damaged. Yet Moravia only limped on an artificial leg, which was more easily acceptable. It was not like an affliction born out of an inferno.

Still, it was because of Moravia's understanding that

the pilot had been hired. Moravia did not believe a pretty face or a formal education was a necessary requirement for a man who flew the mails. He wanted men who could take care of themselves.

MORAVIA was superintendent of the line. The post office was demanding of companies awarded a mail contract and Moravia knew his route was the most difficult of all. It was Moravia's affair to keep the eight pilots who did the actual flying at their task and reasonably happy. In the air, he reasoned, it was their business to keep themselves alive, yet he knew he held the power of life and death over them. He had hired them all and each one was aware as Moravia was aware that if his flying was curtailed the poor man would first wither and eventually die within. Moravia was reluctant to take advantage of his power, but he did not hesitate if a pilot erred.

"One thing. You fly for this company and you stay out of trouble . . . both aloft and on the ground. That is all there is to it. Second thing. You carry on to your destination unless you are absolutely certain the weather is impossible. Otherwise you will be replaced."

Moravia was severe, but he was not unkind. He was sympathetic when a pilot was ill, clucking like a mother hen over his symptoms and admonishing him not to fly if he felt the least chill. "Flying is uncomfortable enough as it is," he said. "If you're shivering with fever, then what will you have left to tell you it is time to be scared?"

Moravia loved his pilots and the very aircraft in which they flew. Yet he was extraordinarily careful that his feeling for both would never be known.

Because of his handicap Moravia had become fat. Photographs taken when he was flying Nieuports in France and had two good legs testified that he had been a dashing youth, if somewhat short and wild of eye, but now he supported a considerable paunch and heavy dew-laps drooped down both sides of his chin. He wore glasses which he so hated he was constantly whipping them on and off the bridge of his nose. He smoked continuously—"Caporals," black tobacco cigarettes which he imported from France at great trouble and considerable expense. Only his voice suggested that he was still a young man. While his eyes were weary his voice was deep and vibrant, almost sonorous in tone. Many people found strange pleasure in listening to Moravia no matter what he was saying.

While they were in flight Moravia did not think of or refer to his pilots by name; instead he employed the company number painted on the tail of the Stearman they were flying.

"Eleven has landed at Baker for more fuel . . . Fourteen has given up and trained the mail at Boise. Goddamn December. Doesn't the sun ever shine any more? . . ."

In Moravia's mind there was no distinct separation between man and aircraft. They were as one. "Seven should change to Nine when he lands. His oil pressure is acting up." When eventually Seven landed, Moravia's orderly mind would see to it that Seven would automatically become Nine.

Now Moravia studied the large wall map which portrayed the tortured and desolate terrain over which his numbers flew. There were great valleys where the flying was relatively easy, but the largest portion of the route was over mountains and high desert, both unforgiving. During the summer the deserts were a bake oven and the little mail planes were tossed about like thistles dancing on the wind. Then, while the heat of the day reigned, the few ranchers remained inside and only the tumbleweed moved across the terrain. In winter cruel winds tore blizzards out of the western ranges and flayed them all along the route between Pasco in Washington and Elko in Nevada. Then even the land shivered.

Moravia was vaguely displeased with what little information he had just received and he tried to ease his suspicions by limping to the window of his simple office and regarding the view. Beyond was the airport or "aerodrome" as he sometimes found himself still referring to it. A wind-sock topped the hangar adjacent to the small structure which housed his office and a cramped area which served as a waiting room for visitors who might have business with the line. It was also a place to stow the mail if either the pick-up truck or an aircraft were tardy. Additionally the area served as a changing room where pilots squirmed into their heavy flight suits if they were about to fly or removed them if they had just landed.

Moravia understood that if a pilot had just arrived he experienced a period of readjustment, a necessary and sometimes unhappy rejoining of themselves with their earthly life. Depending on the man, it took as much as half an hour to shed the peculiar euphoria of flight and to substitute the cares of wife, money, and food for those of wind and cloud. To ease the transformation Moravia had personally installed an electric coffee urn and out of his own pocket bought sweet rolls to complement the refreshment. Whether his pilots appreciated his gesture he cared little. Seeing to their well-being once they had performed, he considered a part of his duty.

Across the field was the metal tower of a rotating beacon which had been recently installed by the government. It flashed a green and then a white light, marking the airport's location for those who sought it at night or in poor visibility. Otherwise there was nothing to see except the flat expanse of prairie now officially designated as an airport and the present heavy grey cloud ceiling above. As he blew smoke at the window, Moravia concentrated on the sky and how the present swift passage of cloud from horizon to horizon might influence further flight operations. And he regretted the limited intelligence that had come to his hand.

One hour previously Moravia had received a telegram advising that Fourteen had taken off from Elko—two hundred pounds of mail and one passenger. Female. The weather had been good with some high stuff. Thin sun visible through same. No problem. Twenty-five degrees. Too cold for snow. Good enough, he thought. The departure had been late because of a "mechanical." No excuse for that. Drop a sharp note to Probosky. And, then, what of the weather situation along the route?

Between Elko and Pasco there was always a void. Boise was the halfway mark and there his airplanes were refueled, the mails resorted, and sometimes pilots were changed for either the north- or southbound flights. Boise weather could not be considered indicative of the entire route. Two hours previously Moravia had telephoned both Boise and Twin Falls for a synopsis of their weather. The ceiling was high and the visibility lower to the west. There were snow squalls visible on the horizon and the wind was variable. Nothing really to provide a sense of certainty.

Better to consult a rancher near Boise who had a good view of the surrounding mountains and, more importantly, had a telephone. He was cooperative and pleasant about giving local weather reports, and to express his gratitude Moravia occasionally sent him a bottle of whiskey smuggled down from Canada. But this morning there had been no answer to the ranch phone's persistent ringing.

So much for the weather in between, Moravia thought. He detested clichés yet now he found one at least partly satisfying. "Ignorance is bliss," he muttered at the window.

Moravia reminded himself that Fourteen was a good

and wise pilot. There was nothing to be concerned about.

Still, sucking on his cigarette, Moravia decided that he did not like the smell of things this morning. There were too many vagaries and that was unfair. He should not have to send his pilots into uncertainties. That smacked of transferring the burden from them to him.

THE pilot eased his weight off the parachute seat momentarily and moved his gun holster further forward on his belt. He considered the gun a nuisance, a hangover from pony-express days when bandits were supposed to be always after the mail. The gun was a relatively small calibre, a .38 automatic which the pilot had never fired. But carrying a gun to protect the mails was Post Office regulation and Moravia saw to it there were no infractions. He was deaf to entreaties that the gun would be almost useless should anyone go down; that a man needed a rifle to hit anything in the wilderness. "You will wear the gun because the Post Office says you will. Bureaucrats are very sensitive people and I do not want inspectors sniffing around here and finding we fail to take them seriously."

Apparently every mail contractor in America felt the same way, for the ever present gun had become the badge of an air-mail pilot throughout the land. Most of them thought wearing the gun in these tranquil times was ridiculous.

Moravia's pilots held mixed feelings about the extra paraphernalia he insisted must be part of their personal gear. In addition to a knife he decreed they must carry a pair of pliers, a small crescent wrench, and a screwdriver. "And if I were you," he said in a voice that offered little option, "I would also carry pain pills. There was a time when I would have given my soul for just one."

15

Now somehow the gun had worked itself around until it prodded the pilot in the ribs and he thought, as he had many times before, that he would like to throw it over the side. "I'm going to be held up? Up *here?*"

When he was settled again he took off his glove and reached into the knee-pocket of his teddy bear. He found his pocket knife and separated it from the chocolate bar he always carried should he feel the need of fresh energy. Then he remembered he was searching in the wrong pocket. The chewing gum he sought was in the other knee-pocket along with those items he thought might ease the stress of a forced landing. There was a box of matches that he carried, although he did not smoke; damned handy to build fires if marooned almost anywhere along the route. Seeking the gum, he fingered the miniature bottle of iodine, a roll of gauze and adhesive tape, and a package of pain-relieving pills.

Every airman had his own version of what might come in handy if a forced landing became necessary. A few carried a flask of whiskey and were often the target of amusement because of it. Were they not aware that wherever in the wilderness they might go down they need not suffer long? A moonshiner's still would be near by.

The pilot preferred to hold his emergency items to a minimum and use the pocket space for a thin leather notebook that he up-dated with meticulous care. Each page offered a diagram of the most likely fields and pastures along the route in which he might make an emergency landing. The altitudes, lengths, and surface characteristics were carefully recorded.

He had also drawn in the surrounding hazards, a clump of high trees along this side of a field, a power line here, a water tower which was conspicuous from the south only. Elsewhere in the notebook were separate pages of each of the few airports within the Stearman's limited range. He had drawn arrowed lines illustrating

16

what experience had taught him was the best approach in bad weather. Fly up the canyon until passing over the pond with a beaver dam at one end. Continue for one minute ten seconds, make steep left turn and go back to canyon. Turn right at entrance to canyon, fly ninety degrees for eighty seconds. Good meadow for landing. Ten-mile walk to telephone at Brogan.

He knew how events could multiply very rapidly in bad weather, and since he could not look out of the cockpit, fly, and check his watch at the same time, the pilot had trained himself to count the passing seconds by intermittently pressing his tongue against the roof of his mouth.

The notebook listed many other items, and its compilation had won considerable respect for the pilot among his fellows. They knew it represented much work and they made private excuses for themselves, saying they carried all such information in their heads. A few had started their own notebooks, but most were incomplete and the pilot thought he knew why. They were married or had many friends of both sexes. They would not understand why it was so necessary for a man who was so rarely in the company of other human beings to keep his evenings busy.

The pilot withdrew the packet of gum and reached out again into the slip-stream. He tapped the helmet of his passenger. She turned and smiled as she saw the gum. She pulled out a piece and said "Thank you" with her lips and the pilot marveled at his pleasure in such a simple exchange. Maybe a spoiled little brat, but at least she knew how to smile. And she was spunky, he thought, her own mistress. He had not noticed the slightest hesitation in her voice or manner. She seemed to know exactly what she wanted to say before she uttered a word.

Holding the control stick between his knees he removed his other glove and peeled the paper from a piece of gum. He stuck it between his teeth and as he chewed he thought that his life aloft was very good. Here, at altitude, he knew a sense of well-being he would not have dared elsewhere.

Ever since the crash and the terrible flames he had been haunted by an insidious sense of failure. At times it came on him like a flowing river and he brooded until at last the river ran dry. His student had died in the crash and there was no redemption. Early on, the student had displayed a lack of natural flying talent. He should have been "washed out" rather than encouraged because he was a pleasant and eager young man. Lesson learned by his instructor! In the flying business, kindness could kill.

If the little girl seemed to be so much her own mistress, he thought, then doubt was still his master. How many thousand times had he reviewed every detail and always returned to the same ugly answer? He should have prevented the tragedy—somehow. Exactly what he might have done still eluded him, but the guilt would not go away simply because a committee of men who were not present during the calamity later declared it was not his fault.

The wind had been strong and perhaps the Base Commander should have cancelled all training, but who was in charge of the only aircraft that crashed?

A gust of wind caught the "Jennie" just as the student was flaring for his fifth landing of the day. A wingtip caught the ground—the "Jennie" cart-wheeled and came to pieces as was their nasty habit. Then there was only the flame, dust in his mouth, and a mixed vision of people in brown uniforms running.

It struck the pilot as odd that almost eight years afterward he felt confident in the sky and still, once he became an earthling, he seemed to be a born loser.

This morning the pilot decided to deviate from the usual route northward to Boise. There were roads both to the east and west which were navigation references along the way. The mountains were highest to the east.

Once he had passed over the mine at Tuscarora the pilot saw the whole range was shrouded in heavy cloud and he knew there would be little chance of getting through. The Santa Rosa range which projected along the western side of the plateau displayed an occasional break in the cloud, and doubtless he might work his way through the pass north of Winnemucca. Yet that was the long way around and he saw no need to attempt it.

Directly ahead, above an enormous high plateau which covered a junction of the Oregon, Idaho, Nevada boundaries, the weather was relatively bright and the separation between earth and cloud more than adequate. The pilot was certain that he would be able to get around the scattered snow squalls with only minor detours. Thus he carried on, passing two ranches he recognized.

Far ahead he could see a rumpling of the land, and beyond hunkered a dark gash in the plateau which he knew had been cut by the Owyhee River. If he held his present compass course he must pass over the Little Fork of the Owyhee and then, say half an hour later, he could start letting down into the lower country around Rome. Once past Rome there was a road he could follow northeastward and eventually come out near Boise. The rest would be easy.

He rocked the Stearman's wings gently. Heather turned to look back at him, her blue-green eyes asking if something was wrong. He made a rapid gesture downward with his right hand, pointing at a clearing below. She peered over the side of the cockpit and saw the herd of antelope he had wanted her to see. Her look of delight as they ran before the sound of the engine rewarded him beyond measure.

He thought, Why am I so anxious to please her? If I could snap my fingers and call out a herd of elephants, I would . . . anything to turn the warmth of that face back on me.

Suddenly, reflected in the glass covering the altimeter, he caught a glimpse of his own face. He looked away instantly. And for several minutes afterward he sat immobilized, listening to the steady drumming of the engine. Soon his brooding was relieved by duty. An hour had passed since take-off and now a low scum of cloud covered the terrain. He had watched it slip in gradually, a feathery mantle laced to increasingly numerous snow squalls.

The pilot became busy with choices. Fly around that squall to the northwest say three miles, then turn back northeast on the back side for an equal amount of time. Then once again settle on course. That big hooligan, a grandfather of squalls, could be avoided by another westerly heading—as long as it remained isolated. Be wary though if it joined with too many of its neighbors now multiplying along the horizon. If they became a solid wall, then think about turning back to Elko.

Moravia would not like that, although the pilot now found to his surprise that what his superior might think was not of primary importance. Would turning back disappoint his passenger? Come on! Since when did little girls decide the course of aircraft?

He was watching the parade of squalls dragging a white veil of snow along the surface of the plateau when he first smelled the musky odor of over-heated oil.

He sniffed at the slip-stream. Was he imagining the smell? He tried to smile, reminding himself that engines had a habit of developing "automatic rough" when over hostile terrain. He thought it must be the very first aeronautical joke. Yet—

He pushed his head into the hard slip-stream, looking for oil along the fuselage or engine cowling. Nothing.

He glanced at the oil-pressure gauge. He saw it had slipped down from normal. Yet only a few pounds. Perhaps the oil-cooling system was jammed somehow.

He waited, uneasy with the moment. He looked back over the Stearman's tail. Clear enough from where he had come. A few snow squalls widely separated. Even a thin shaft of sunlight stabbing down through the overcast. A return to Elko would be easy. Have Probosky check the engine again. Maybe a valve sticking, a needed adjustment to the carburetor, water in the fuel . . . something.

Still, if Probosky found nothing wrong? If he handed down his supreme opinion as only Probosky could do: "You hear little fairies singing maybe? You day-dream up there? That engine runs like a sewing machine."

The pilot knew what Probosky would think and what eventually, if he found cause to return too many times for obscure reasons, what other employees of the line would be thinking. And it would not be long afterward that Moravia would be checking his record of trips without incident. How to explain an engine which ran smoothly when all the experts were gathered around it, and had the fits when you were high and alone?

He glanced down at his gloved hand on the control stick. He took off his right glove to better feel any unusual vibration in the control stick. Yes, there was some, but had it not always been so? Why was he now so persuaded there was more vibration than normal? Precisely why? Moravia wanted solid thinkers in his cockpits, not fanciers. Was the smell stronger now? Or was it just fancy?

He glanced at the instrument panel. The oil pressure seemed the same, but the glass covering the instrument was trembling enough to multiply a partial reflection of his helmet.

He pushed up his goggles studying the instruments one by one. He reached out and pressed his hand against the panel trying to steady it. No question. The thunder of the engine remained steady, but the vibration was increasing.

No question? There was a riling in his stomach. His whole body tensed. Here! Of all places.

He looked down and started a turn. He eased back

21

slightly on the throttle. Perhaps if the engine were straining less it would hold together until he could return to Elko. At least until they were near something, for below was only a vast wilderness.

Surprised at the steep banking of the Stearman the girl turned to look back at him. He sought to reassure her.

"Don't worry!" he yelled, but his voice was lost in the roar of the slip-stream and the engine.

Suddenly the Stearman shook violently. The spasm continued for several seconds, then the whole aircraft shuddered mightily as if fighting for its life. The pilot saw the instrument panel shake itself into a blur and a fountain of black smoke enveloped the fuselage.

He cut the throttle immediately, then the fuel mixture, and the magneto switch. He kicked hard right rudder, dipped the left wing to slip away from the smoke, and eased the nose down. The roar of the slip-stream diminished rapidly until there was only the low humming of the flying wires.

"We have to land. Don't worry!"

The pilot was unbelieving. This happens here? The finest engine in the flying world has packed up over one of the worst places in the world?

Gliding down, holding the airspeed at a mere sixty miles per hour, he knew a momentary sense of insult. How dare such fine piece of machinery choose this awkward time to disappoint him?

The pilot began to count those few weapons remaining to him. He estimated his height above the overcast at a thousand feet, which translated into a grace period of perhaps four minutes if he squeezed the maximum time from the glide. There was a hole in the overcast only a mile or so away. He had no idea of the actual height of the terrain, although judging from the fringes of the hole there was very little space between cloud and earth. If any.

He eased up on the ailerons, keeping the bank as

shallow as possible while turning for the hole. More time that way.

The smoke had disappeared soon after he had shut down the engine and for a moment he considered trying to start it up again. Wishful thinking, he knew. And wrong. If he did succeed in starting the engine, then it might vibrate itself right off the mounts and that would most certainly be the end of everything.

He saw the girl was looking back at him and he managed a smile. He heard her call out, "I'm not afraid."

In that instant his resolve took command of his thinking. Somehow he must bring his machine to earth so gently that Heather would not be harmed.

Below, the cloud layer revolved slowly, as if it were turning and the airplane were still. The pilot looked to the south where Elko would be, then promised himself not to look that way again. Even thinking of an easy landing now was distracting and might dull the keen edge of alertness he needed.

He charged himself deliberately, every muscle and nerve waiting for opportunity. Now the Stearman was directly above the hole, circling, descending at absolute minimum speed and yet fast enough to avoid a stall. The more the pilot studied the depths of the hole the more apprehensive he became. He saw nothing but rocks and trees projecting from patches of snow.

He thought, welcome to the side of a mountain. He estimated the incline at the base of the hole to be as much as twenty degrees. He searched the horizon for another hole. Somewhere there must be one with a more inviting interior, but he saw nothing within range of his glide. Time as in a dream, he thought. How leisurely did time pass when there was only one choice.

Looking everywhere his eyes finally met those of his passenger. She was questioning, yet he saw that she was not afraid and he thought how much worse it might have been if his passenger had been an adult who by now would probably be near panic. The little ones are not so afraid of the unfamiliar, he thought, because to them so many things are unfamiliar.

He saw she was waiting patiently for him to do something and that her confidence was total. Did you tell those eyes that no aviator could land down there without smashing something? Did you say, "The purpose of this flight is to deliver the mail. Your pilot was not thinking of you when he flew this direct route over the plateau. It will do no good to complain to the Postmaster General, or even to a man named Moravia"?

He looked away from her eyes long enough to make one last search for another way to descend.

He called out, "Get down as far as you can between the mail sacks!"

She smiled as if she knew exactly why he wanted her to comply and after a moment only the top of her helmet was visible to him.

"Treat her easy, God," he murmured as the Stearman sank to the cloud level. Just as he slipped into the hole and began the final descent, the whole aircraft shuddering at the odd angle it was asked to fly, he remembered in a flash that he was the prime subject in the standard objection most mail pilots had to flying passengers. Alone and in serious trouble, they had only to bail out and float safely to earth. Now he was pleased that he had forgotten he was wearing a parachute.

Two minutes later the details of the mountainside were visible. As the rocks and trees and bush rushed upward, the low vibrato of the flying wires seemed to climb higher in pitch.

There was a clear space. It was not nearly long enough for a normal landing, but it was something to aim at. Two pines stood in the way of a clear entrance to the space. He must slip between them. Knocking the wings off might slow the Stearman's fuselage enough to survive.

He held the side-slip until the very last instant, until he could see the cascades of shale mounded about the rocks. Then he brought the Stearman's nose up, kicked full right rudder to lift out of the slip, and waited. He pulled the control stick as far back as possible and braced one hand against the leather around the cockpit cowling.

The flying wires sighed and then there was only a stunning dissonance of metal against stone and the flat shrieking of torn wood. The pilot closed his eyes and almost immediately afterward knew a tumbling sensation.

MORAVIA sucked deeply on his Caporal while he reviewed the flight report for the previous month. Considering it reflected operations for the month of November which invariably presented weather problems, the report was not bad. The Post Office would be pleased and the executive types who employed him should be satisfied along with the stockholders. There would be very little profit of course. No one who was realistic about the flying business dared to expect true profit.

At least, Moravia thought, we are temporarily out of the red. Or so the bookkeeper claimed. Which was more than most companies doing the same thing could say.

"A hand-to-mouth business," Moravia cautioned all investors who came to him with dreams of getting in on the ground floor of an industry which would soon be carrying tremendous loads of cargo. He remembered a few who predicted a glorious future when air-borne vehicles began carrying such commodities as coal and iron ore.

Lovely, Moravia thought. Our present problem is to get enough mail load to make it worthwhile each way.

Like other operators flying the mail under contract, Moravia sometimes found it necessary to mail a few telephone books back and forth. The Post Office paid by weight. Pilots and mechanics had to be paid and there was his own modest salary to be remembered.

Moravia's mind drifted to more personal affairs. After ten years in the flying business where did he stand? On one leg, of course, but he had yet to miss a meal and there had always been a comfortable roof over his head and his divine Marsha's. So not too bad if certain inevitable cares were set aside.

He fell to thinking of Number Fourteen, who was even now aloft bringing the mails from Elko to Boise. Fourteen, he thought, was in some ways a man to be envied although he would certainly disagree if challenged. He lived alone, a man without apparent cares. When he descended from his daily work he could do as he pleased—go to the movies or a speakeasy, or he could just go back to his room and read the *Literary Digest* or lie down and rest without thinking about what was happening to his comrades on the line. If he looked out the window and saw that it was lousy weather he could just say to himself, "Well, I did my chore for the day and here I am all warm and my ass is entirely safe and who cares what happens the rest of the day?"

That was the way Number Fourteen would be privileged to think, once he had two feet on the ground.

Moravia grunted. Would he trade places? Even with that face? The answer, he decided, was yes and no. Fourteen was a free agent, all right; he left his work behind him when he went home. But what kind of a home waited for him when he went up those steps behind a hardware store and turned into that single room? Moravia had been there once when Fourteen suffered a severe case of bronchitis. Moravia had brought him the newspapers and a copy of *Aero Digest,* which carried an article on the new Tri-Motored Fords. "Someday," he had told Fourteen, "I suppose we'll be flying those machines on the line and I thought you'd like to learn something about them."

But Fourteen had turned his head to the wall, keeping the good side of his face toward Moravia, and he had said he hoped it would be a long time before carrying passengers would become a regular thing. And Moravia was sure he was thinking about his face and how difficult it would be for him to present himself before any assembly of people. Fourteen's appearance was accepted here, Moravia was reminded, but among strangers he collided with an awkward problem. The bad side of his mouth offered a sort of permanent snarl which was enough to discourage the most friendly overtures. Therefore, Moravia decided, the man's almost complete isolation. Therefore, his monastic room, so barren of personal reflection it could have been a monk's cell. There was his bed which reminded Moravia of the cot he had been assigned when he had flown in France. There was a wooden bureau which Moravia assumed held his shirts, socks, and underwear. One drab brown suit hung on a rod which stretched between the wash-basin and the door. There was also a single pair of slacks and the usual hard-worn leather jacket, which nearly all pilots wore like a second skin. The bath, Moravia assumed, was down the hall.

There was a telephone on top of the bureau and nothing more. The telephone was a company regulation and Moravia found himself wondering if it ever rang except for a call from himself.

The only clue to the inner man that Moravia had so far been able to discover had been through a chance conversation with the local librarian who was a friend of Marsha's. "He treats books as if they were living creatures," she reported. "He reads everything from *Seven Pillars of Wisdom* to Maugham. Once I asked him how he liked Henry James. He said, 'Over-rated.' That is the longest speech I've ever heard him make."

Now, as he glowered at the heavy sky through his office window, Moravia knew he would not trade places with Fourteen. It could be no great pleasure to be a free agent when you limited your own freedom—or events had destroyed any hope of a woman's love. Indeed, what would Fourteen do but turn his face the other way, being careful to position himself so there always was something between the rest of the world and his misfortune. A man could do very well without a leg, Moravia reminded himself, as witness his own marriage. Yet even Marsha, whose tolerance and sympathies flowed from her, found it difficult not to flinch when by chance she encountered Fourteen.

Moravia was amused to discover he was thinking of love on this Tuesday morning at ten thirty-three. And in his office of all places! Perhaps he should ring Marsha and advise her how her peglegged mate had this morning also lost half his wits. "Good morning, Mrs. Moravia. Please be alerted that I have banished thinking of the mail this morning and am devoting myself to the matter of love. I have concluded it cannot flourish for long in an atmosphere of seclusion and I have been further reminded that there are a great many people who remain solitary though they may be surrounded by others. With that dreary acorn I will say goodbye, Mrs. Moravia, and wish you a more pleasant day than I anticipate for myself."

Moravia went to the phone, but he did not call his wife. He hoped to find the rancher who might give him the latest weather to the west of Boise. He listened to the ringing sound for a long time before he became convinced there would be no response.

* * *

THE pilot licked his lips and tasted oil. He rubbed at his mouth with the back of his gloved hand and opened his eyes. He saw the familiar rim of the cockpit but it did not look at all the same. The windscreen was opaque instead of transparent and for a moment he studied the cobweb pattern of cracks in the glass. Then suddenly he realized what was wrong. He was lying on his side with his head resting on a pile of shale. The entire fuselage lay on its side and he was still strapped in his seat.

His thoughts were feathery. The leg straps of his parachute were pinching his groin, but the pain was insignificant compared to the wonder he found in realizing that the bad side of his face, the same side which had been his curse for so long, was now once again pressed hard against the planet earth. The realization eluded him, then returned, and his mind laughed. Some landing, old sport, one of your better performances, I might say. Why don't you try the other side next time? Anyone can land right side up.

Then suddenly he remembered he was not alone.

His thoughts congealed as a chill ran through his body. He reached quickly for his safety belt and opened the clip. Then his fingers found the snaps to his parachute harness. His headache vanished as he squirmed out of the cockpit and brought himself to his knees.

He waited a moment, trying to assure himself that what he saw was not real. The crumpled wings of the Stearman were embracing two trees more than fifty yards away. In between there was a wheel and a tire, a piece of propeller, and two bags of mail. One had burst and its contents formed a path to the Stearman's tail, which was intact except for the crushed elevator and horizontal stabilizer on the down side. The fuselage was bent and wrinkled but not badly damaged between the cockpit and the tail.

As he stared at the wreckage his thoughts became patchy again just long enough for him to decide that

Moravia would be pleased. The cost of repair would be minimal. Then he realized there would never be any repairs.

He caught his breath as his eyes focused on the mail bin, which was normally sheltered beneath the upper wing. A long moment passed before he could recognize what he was looking at. The center section struts were bent back and lay almost flat against some dun-colored mail sacks. He noted the sacks were smeared with oil and he thought the Post Office department would be unhappy. He would tell them: "Well, what the hell can you expect when they've had a big fat thousand-pound engine lying right on top of them?"

The engine was bent back and out of its mounts, twisted on its side at a crazy angle. Otherwise, he thought, it looked fine. Just wipe off a little oil here and there and probably the engine could be sold almost as good as new . . . except for a few things, of course. Like a rather poor record for behavior—?

A sound punctured his errant thought. The sound tore through his ears and left him gasping at his confusion. The girl . . . Heather! The faint little cry told him she was just there, a few feet from him, buried beneath the center section, somewhere under the sacks and the engine.

He rose, staggered a few feet, then lunged at the engine. He heard his own voice, but it seemed to be that of some ventriloquist calling from far away. "Oh God. *Please* don't let her be hurt! I will give you my life if she is not hurt."

He spoke to the pile of junk that had been Number Fourteen airplane as if it could respond.

"Don't worry, girl. I'll have you out of there in a jiffy. Just be patient with me." He was angry at his inability to remember her name.

His only answer was the faint cry, so small and fragile he thought she sounded more like a just-hatched bird.

Tearing at a mail sack with all his strength failed to move it from beneath the engine. He saw her foot extending from beneath another mail sack and he thought, maybe, just maybe, this is good. Oh God, please.

"Listen, girl." What the hell was her name? "I have to move the engine off the sacks. It's very heavy and I have to find something to pry with. Maybe it will take me a few minutes to find something. Please, just wait please."

He turned away from the wreckage, stumbling and slipping on the shale and trying to remember the little girl's name. He followed a straight and shallow trench which he realized had been dug by the fuselage as it slid to a stop.

He decided that he had done an acceptable job of hitting the two trees in such a way the wings were knocked off simultaneously. He had avoided a slew which at that speed might have killed them both. They would have hit the mountain at an angle. As it was they had grafted on to it. The trench could have been drawn on a ruler, he thought. The Stearman's speed had been decelerated relatively smoothly and while it made a hell of a mess it seemed that no one was badly hurt. Any landing you could walk away from was better than an uncontrolled crash. So they said. And right. The girl's name was Heather.

He found a broken branch hanging from one of the trees and yanked at it until it came away. With it fell soft loaves of snow which struck him in the face and refreshed him. As he dragged the branch back across the shale he avoided looking at the wreckage. If the truth were known, he thought unhappily, he had *not* done things right. If he had just flown the regular route instead of bearing off to the west and the same thing had happened, then he would have had much flatter terrain for an emergency landing. Probably all of Moravia's other pilots would have maintained the regular course come no matter what . . . or they would have turned back, landed, and done their explaining and maybe even the engine would have held up until they actually landed at Elko. Now Moravia was minus one whole airplane which could never be put back together again. Like Humpty-Dumpty, he thought.

When he had arrived back at the fuselage he paused and tried to recover from a new sensation of dizziness which seemed to come and go in waves. He looked down toward the base of the mountain and saw only patches of forest beneath a grey layer of cloud. We will need water, he thought, and almost simultaneously congratulated himself on doing something right. Telling the little girl to get down under the mail sacks had probably saved her life. Probably. He would point that out to her because, he warned himself, this whole thing was going to be very difficult to explain to those eyes of hers and he would need all the credit he could manage. God almighty, weren't her parents aware that flying was not exactly safe and that maybe a thing like this *could* happen and then where would their daughter be?

God almighty . . . Please don't let her be hurt!

He fought off his vertigo and shoved one end of the branch between the shale and the bottom cylinder of the engine. He pried with all his strength, then rested while he tried to drive the confusion from his thoughts. This was impossible. Four men might move the engine, but one tired aviator heaving on the end of a pine branch . . . well, it was obviously hopeless. Who are you? he asked himself. Samson?

He heaved on the branch once more and saw the engine tilt slightly. Or was it just his imagination? If he had a longer branch he could get more leverage, yet because of the slope of the mountain he would not be able to use the extra length. He moved around to the front of the fuselage where the engine would normally be, and told himself to start using his brain instead of his back.

He descended to his knees and started pawing at the shale. Perhaps if he worked hard enough he could dig out beneath the wreckage . . . enough to reach beneath the mail sacks and pull them away. First things first. That is, before—?

The shale made a clicking sound as it slithered away from his hands and down the slope. Here I am, he thought, scratching away at a mountain like an animal. This was not part of my flight training. They should tell people who say they love to fly that someday if they are stupid, and have the talent for doing the wrong thing at the right time, they will wind up on their hands and knees trying to dig a hole in the side of a mountain. He halted his efforts when he had removed only a few inches of shale. He had come to bed rock. He listened and when the chittering noise of the shale ceased somewhere far below there was only the sound of his own heavy breathing. "Heather?" he asked softly, "can you hear me?"

The silence shocked him. No, no. She was all right. She *must* be all right.

He pushed himself slowly to his feet, wondering if he dared call her name again. Now wait a minute, God. I botched things, but enough is enough.

He moved around to the branch again, stepping cautiously on the shale lest he miss the slightest sound from the mail bin. A wild thought occurred to him. Maybe if he told her the situation she could dig herself out, kick the mail sacks away? Should he say, as if he really believed it, "Listen, little Heather. I need your help to get you out of there because we have a lot to do before it gets dark. We have to build some kind of shelter and wait for the weather to clear. Then we can walk down the mountain and that's all there will be to it."

He stood staring at the engine as if it were alive, and it was some time before he realized the faint peckling sound he heard was the touching of snowflakes on the drum-tight fabric of the fuselage. He busied his hands removing the belt which held his airmail gun. It had become surprisingly heavy and he was about to toss it carelessly away when he decided it might prove useful after all. Maybe if it snowed too hard and they had to stay here a day or two he could shoot something. Heather would be hungry because kids always were.

As he placed the gun carefully on the upturned side of the fuselage he heard a different sound. His whole body seemed to explode.

He listened, then heard it again—a faint whimper. He thought it was an almost unhuman sound and that if he heard it just once more he would go insane.

Yet he waited impatiently for the silence to end. Hating the absolute quiet he was astounded to discover he could feel the beating of his pulse.

He heard a faint cry from the wreckage and instantly forgot the branch and his unsteady footing on the shale. He forgot the silent mountain.

Seething with fury he threw himself at the engine. He seized it by two cylinders and jamming his shoulder against the gear section he pushed and shoved until his blood pounded against his temples and his sight became clouded. He resented the sound of metal scraping against metal. For some reason he could not understand it seemed terribly important that he avoid making any more noise than necessary. His heavy breathing was a giveaway, of course, but he was determined to ignore it. The task was so obviously impossible he must not admit for one second that it was.

He had no idea how long he wrestled with the engine, or whether anything else in the world existed save this monstrous mass of metal, when he sensed that it had shifted position. He fought still harder, lifting and pushing, catching at the oil-smelling air in quick, intermittent gasps, grunting in spite of his desire for silence, every muscle and fiber in his body fully committed to the attack. Then at last he heard a metallic tearing sound and he knew something had given way in the engine mount. He shoved with his final strength and the engine rolled away from the mail sacks. He fell upon it for support, still unbelieving of his victory, sobbing for wind.

Moments later he bent to the mail sacks, heaved them aside and saw his passenger. She was sprawled on her back, strangely twisted, but her eyes were open and he knew she recognized him. He kneeled beside her and brushed the new flakes of snow from her forehead. "You're all right now?"

He waited for the tears he feared would come, but there were none. Instead she stared up at him, her eyes uncertain, and she said, "I don't think so."

"Can you get up if I help you?"

"I don't know." Her eyelids flickered. "I think . . . my back maybe."

He slid one hand behind her neck, then eased the other beneath her leg. Maybe, if she was set on her feet?

He lifted her leg less than half an inch when he saw her eyes close and she screamed in agony.

JUST south of the Black Rock Desert near Winnemucca Lake, the center of the low-pressure area tightened. It moved slowly toward the northeast across the barren mountains and the desolate valleys where only a few stubborn ranchers had learned to exist with the environment. The low sent ahead of it many harbingers in the form of snow squalls which sifted downward in grey-white columns, then gave way to the influence of the terrain and swept onward in graceful curves.

Behind the squalls came the wind, and borne on the gusts were much heavier snows which rapidly enveloped the mountain peaks and transformed the adjacent valleys and canyons into an almost featureless landscape. The ravines were the first to disappear, then the outcroppings which had long before guided both Indians and whites, and finally the smaller streams vanished. Soon there remained only a vast grey emptiness beneath which all of nature slept.

Not even the most knowledgeable rancher would have ventured from his shelter on such a day of snows and wind, into the unfamiliarity of what had once been so familiar. Each in his own way knew from past winters that once this wilderness turned sullen it was not easy for a man to shake loose a feeling of utter helplessness. All very well to place faith in God, but there were times when He chose to display a man's puniness.

THREE hundred miles to the north in Pasco, Moravia's ordered mind was uncomfortable with speculation. He detested not knowing what he thought he should know and it struck him as nearly incredible that in this day and age, in the December of 1928 which was at least one thing he could be specific about, indeed in the supposedly civilized United States of America he could be held in such ignorance of what was going on. The days of Lewis and Clark were long gone, the few Indians who inhabited the land over which his mail planes flew were peaceable, the railroads were built, along with a few good highways, and yet now, he thought, he might as well be a major of Cavalry marooned within a log fort. In fact, he concluded, his boots-and-saddles counterpart might be better informed, with a few galloping troopers to bring him news.

During the past hour Moravia had rung his favorite rancher again and again, always with the same negative results. He found the ringing tone itself discouraging, with its forlorn tune of loneliness, a repetitive monotone that seemed to mock his increasing anxiety. Fourteen was not due to land for another hour and ten minutes so there was nothing to worry about there, but the southbound mail (Number Eight that would be) was due to take off in twenty minutes. His aircraft was ready and Moravia knew he was now passing the time by drinking coffee and munching on the day before yesterday's doughnuts. He was waiting for the arrival of the mail in the Post Office truck. Eight was already in his "teddy bear" although he had not yet buttoned up. Being a wise pilot he was wearing heavy boots and socks to keep his feet warm.

The question now was should Eight go at all? If it became necessary for him to turn around halfway or even sooner and bring the mail back to Pasco, the Postmaster would be extremely unhappy. If the air mail was delayed too many times during the year, then there would be ugly hints of contract cancellation which of course for Moravia and the entire line would mean the end. The alternative was to "train" the mail, an embarrassing confession of incompetence that left the railroads laughing and, Moravia thought ruefully, the bureaucrats convinced they should have relied on the iron horse to begin with.

In good weather, of course, there was no real decision to be made. The morning plane took away the mail at eleven and that was that, although Moravia hoped wistfully there might be a few more and heavier sacks than there ever seemed to be. The trouble was that when the damn train was on time it left the station at eleven forty, which meant that if he delayed his decision beyond, say, ten fifty, the mail might just miss the train. The result was an automatic uproar with everyone mad at everyone else and accusations doing all the flying. The Postmaster would be furious because he would have to write a letter to Washington explaining why his mail was a whole day behind time, and since he dreaded the labor of writing, not to mention fear for

37

his sinecure, he would direct his wrath first at Moravia and then at the railroad. The railroad people would maintain their usual haughty attitude toward Moravia and anything to do with flying machines while at the same time berating the Post Office for not allowing more time between the arrival of the mail at the station and the departure of their precious choo-choo. All a monumental pain in the ass, Moravia thought, as he lit his fifteenth Caporal of the morning.

The heavy, lung-scratching smoke sent him off into a fit of coughing which he thought was at least less annoying than his present and all too frequent dilemma. The flying conditions between Pasco and Elko along the middle of the route were the real villain. His rancher, who must have taken himself to Florida for the winter, would know something of his local weather, but the true need was to know the weather along the entire route. When Fourteen eventually landed he could give a full report, yet whatever he might have to say must be classed as ancient history. It might have been fine for him in the south, but by the time Eight reached the same area things could be stinking. The solution, of course, was direct ground-to-air communication, and Moravia understood there were some experimental radio installations being used by the pilots who flew back east, but successful two-way contacts were so rare it was not worth the cost. Maybe someday.

Maybe someday also the gates of paradise would swing open and reveal at least one banker who thought making progress in the sky was more important than an immediate profit. That same liberated, intelligent, imaginative banker might have been to England and Europe where airplanes were flying all over the place with mail, where between London and Paris and Berlin and Moscow they were carrying as many as fourteen passengers and serving them lunch on white linen tablecloths with wine and all the fixings. No American line had even given serious thought to such things.

Moravia watched the mail truck pull up outside his office window and he noted that it was precisely ten forty. All right. Decision time had come and it was not made easier by the fact that the mail truck appeared to have an unusually heavy load.

"Money," Moravia thought, "inspires the lazy man to achievements he would never dare attempt." He grunted. ". . . and as well," he thought, "does it sour the energies of those who would have done better without it."

Still, he must not toy over-long with such fancy and pleasurable thoughts. He must abandon them in mid-air and keep his good leg rooted in the practical. It was always a good payload that was the hardest to divert.

Moravia expected the knock on his door and its immediate opening. His caller was Manigault, a soft-spoken Carolinian who would want to know what decision Moravia had reached although both men understood the decision was not Moravia's alone to make. If Manigault, who had already become Number Eight in Moravia's thoughts, chose not to fly and his reasons were sound, his was the final word. The code was unwritten, as was the understanding that there would be no penalties or recriminations inflicted upon the reluctant pilot. The code did not apply to those who might repeatedly find reason not to fly. Moravia was well aware that, as in any company of men, he had his rascals and there were a few who might employ dubious weather as an excuse to lie with their latest female conquest. To the best of Moravia's knowledge they had never outwitted him.

Eight was a slight man who looked physically lost in his enormous teddy bear. He was a thorough gentleman, an attribute Moravia appreciated.

Manigault asked, "Do I earn my keep today?"

"It's up to you. Elko is fine . . . two thousand and ten with snow squalls. Boise has a good ceiling and visibility between snow squalls, but I can't find out what you'll have en route."

Manigault bent slightly for a better view out the window. Then, as if he could actually see beyond the horizon, he said, "It looks okay. I'll sneak around things . . . if there is anything."

"Keep your eye out for Fourteen. You should pass him somewhere around Baker."

Manigault pulled his helmet and goggles from under his arm and clapped them carelessly on his head. As he buttoned up his teddy bear he said, "Sometimes I wish I were back in Carolina. You start out the day there and you know pretty well how the rest of the day will go. But in this country—"

Manigault left his sentence unfinished and Moravia knew why. It was his own intolerance of complaint, and Manigault was aware of it as were all the others. His pilots were *flying,* which to a certain breed of man was as necessary as breathing. They did not know what it was like to be denied the privilege as Moravia had been, but by God if they grumbled about anything at all they knew they could expect a tart lecture on their mortal values. They would be reminded of the averages, which indicated without equivocation that flying the mails was not for babies. They would also be reminded that more than forty pilots had been killed flying the mails, and twenty-three seriously injured since the service began. Of course if they preferred to lead the life of butchers, bakers, or candlestick makers Moravia would be glad to show them the door and offer them a souvenir hook for the hanging of their helmet and goggles. Now, flying the mails was no longer a government affair. This year for the first time private operators were doing the job and Moravia intended to prove that on his part at least the dubious safety record could be improved.

Instead of wasting their wind complaining, Moravia had urged his men to expend the same effort in learning every stream, rock, mountain, and glade along their route. An accumulation of such knowledge just might prove beneficial to their health when the sketchy road maps they used for navigation ran out of information.

"If you will give me your two legs then I will tune my two ears to your complaint," Moravia was fond of saying. "But my sympathies are hard to arouse if you kill yourself with some foolishness. Be assured my letter to your survivors will be truthful instead of laudatory. Do not oblige me to write he was so busy finding fault with every little thing that he failed to perceive the faults within himself. So the dunce flew into a rock-lined cloud."

IT was nearly dusk before the pilot had done all he thought he had to do. The terrible sound of his passenger's screaming still echoed in his ears and he had resolved after a second attempt to abandon any hope of moving her out of the wreckage until help was available. As long as she remained still she seemed comfortable enough, but something was grievously wrong with her back and the slightest movement became obvious torture.

He had decided he must build their shelter around Heather rather than trying to move her to a better location. He had arranged the mail bags into a sort of foundation and although they smelled of oil and gasoline they provided an efficient barrier against the drifting snow. All during the afternoon the snow had increased until now, as he completed his work, he waded in it up to his knees.

He had cut large sections of fabric off the Stearman's broken wings, tied down the ends with shale and rocks, and stretched them over the twisted fuselage. He had opened his parachute and draped the silk over the tail and engine. The result was a crude tent which he thought might even be considered as cozy under different circumstances.

It was almost dark when he stood back and surveyed his handiwork. For a moment the sight of such a flimsy structure nearly overwhelmed his resolve. He saw that even a moderate wind would blow the whole crazy thing away and he wondered how so little could have been accomplished after so much hard labor.

He told himself it was certainly the altitude which had brought on his exhaustion. Now he thought he knew the truth. His barely controllable weariness, this yearning just to lie down and go to sleep, was the sum of his fears. For now that the physical work was temporarily done he had at last made himself look at their true situation. And what he saw was dismaying.

He stood in snow which was rapidly becoming deeper. The snow blanketed a Nevada mountain, or was it actually in Nevada? Perhaps they had flown further than he realized and crossed into Idaho. He had no idea of the mountain's name or what access there might be to lower lands, or if there was any nearby civilization. He was aware that he was approximately one hour's flying time from Elko, a morsel of knowledge which was presently not of much value.

He was a stranger lost in hostile land. For company he had a helpless little girl whose eyes declared she trusted him with their future. There was no escaping those eyes; they said, "I know we are in deep trouble, but you will find a way out of it."

At least, he thought, Moravia would now be certain that he was missing and would have already organized a search. But where would his searchers search except along the usual route, which would not bring them this way?

The pilot looked up at the trees which clung to the steep side of the mountain and wondered how they could grow in such an environment. He saw that the same trees would render him nearly invisible from the air; unless an airplane flew directly over the site and the pilot happened to be looking down at just the right instant. Even the wreckage would be very difficult to spot—the parts of a dead insect scattered beneath the snow. The long track made by the sliding fuselage had already vanished.

The pilot paused beside the fuselage while he counted his total assets. There was his one bar of chocolate, which he thought to feed Heather in small amounts. In the dark there was no reason for her to know he was not consuming a like amount. A piece of gum would ease his appetite and there were four left in the packet. There was a full box of matches, but he had been able to gather very little wood. Tomorrow he hoped to explore further.

He had given one of the pain pills to Heather and there were nine left. He had used half the little bottle of iodine swabbing at the small cuts on Heather's face and upon his own left arm, which bore an ugly gash. Somehow the sleeve of his teddy bear had been pushed up during impact and the shale had cut into his flesh. Yet such was his concern for Heather he had not noticed the wound until long after the crash. Now it was well wrapped in gauze and had stopped bleeding. His forearm was still numb, but he knew it was not broken. Lucky.

He sank to his knees in the snow and crawled inside the shelter. The last of the daylight filtered through the parachute cloth and fabric and he saw that Heather's eyes were open. "I thought you would be asleep."

She made no reply and he thought that if she let one tear go he would have to find some excuse to go outside for a while. "Do you realize that you are probably the only girl in the world with your very own silken tent?"

She looked at him steadily and he longed to know exactly what she was thinking. Were those eyes accusing him? Or were they nearly expressionless because of the pain pill?

"Do you hurt now?"

She shook her head ever so slightly.

"Is there anything I can do to make you more comfortable?"

"I'm cold."

He took off his teddy bear and moving very carefully, tucked it around her. She protested, saying softly that now he would be cold and she would not want him to be. "I'm actually too hot. I've been getting us organized."

"Could we have a fire if we're going to camp out all night?"

All night? They would be very lucky if help came within a week. He explained that he would not build a fire inside their tent since the airplane's fuel tank was still in place and leaking slowly. He told her that if she could smell gasoline fumes not to worry. And maybe in the morning he could separate the fuel tank from the center section . . . somehow.

"Just for tonight I'll build our fire outside so we can melt some snow for water. And now for the menu. The entree is a special chocolate pudding which you can wash down with snow champagne. Dessert if you are good might even be a piece of gum."

A silence fell between them. The pilot listened to the ticking of snow above his head and thought that it was going to be a very long night.

Now it was dark inside the shelter. He pulled off his gloves and feeling in the knee-pocket of his teddy bear he found the chocolate bar. He broke off a piece and reached out in the darkness for Heather's hand. "Here's dinner. Eat slowly and it will last longer. And be sure to fold your napkin afterward."

He heard her chewing and when she had finished she said, "You are a good cook."

"It may not be like your mother would make, but it will have to do for now."

"My mother will be worried. Will someone look for us?"

"Yes."

"Tonight? They can't find us at night, can they?"

"No. Tomorrow at first light they'll be looking." The pilot could see them—all six airplanes of the line and probably some from the National Guard. Yet he saw them to the east, sashaying back and forth across the sky, covering the regular route, but they would not be looking in the right area. "Probably," he said, wondering how he could lie so easily, "probably they will find us tomorrow."

"Then what?"

Indeed. Then what? "Probably some rangers or trappers or ranchers . . . or someone who knows this country, will come after us."

"If I could move we could go down the mountain by ourselves. I'm all right as long as I stay perfectly still . . . but when I move even a teensy bit . . . well . . ."

"You'll be much better tomorrow."

"I hope so. Can I tell you something? Sort of confidential?"

"I'm your best and only listener. And my lips are sealed."

"I have to go . . ."

"You mean?"

"Uh-huh."

"Oh. Well, now . . . just hold everything a minute. I should have thought." He fumbled for his gloves, found them, and crawled outside. Somewhere in the line of wreckage, he remembered, there was a section of metal cowling. Normally it was fitted between the fuselage and the engine, but it had been separated and badly bent by the impact.

He waded through the snow along where he thought the trail should be. He went all the way to the crumbled wings and halfway back to the shelter before his boot slid over something hard. He reached down and pulled up the piece of cowling he had wanted. Laboring in the darkness he placed the metal beneath one knee and forced his weight downward until he bent it more. His fingers worked as if he were blind and in time they became numb, but he knew he had managed to twist and bend the metal until he had formed a crude pan. He took it to the shelter and crawled inside.

"Hello," he said, "you have a visitor."

"Who is it?"

"Me. The duty nurse. Were you expecting anyone else? Now if you will just bite a bullet and let me ease this under . . ."

Fumbling cautiously in the darkness he heard her gasp several times, but at last she lay quietly and he asked if he could remove the pan. "Yes," she whispered, "I am so embarrassed."

"Don't be. I am your friend."

As he crawled toward the exit he heard her say very softly, "Thank you. You are a very beautiful person."

And he was glad it was so dark.

Later he lay down beside her, sensing her closeness instinctively. He believed she was asleep so he kept his silence and tried not to think about their situation. Tomorrow, he thought, would be a new day and his head might not ache and he would be able to concentrate on getting off the mountain.

He could not sleep. Armies of thoughts marched across his mind. Why had he given so much of his life to flying? Very few businessmen died at their desks and very few farmers were run over and smashed by their tractors. It was unlikely that a lawyer or a merchant might be consumed by fire or frightened half out of their wits several times a year.

Flying paid well, but he could not think of a pilot who flew just for the money. Some of the pilots he knew were a little odd in their ways. It was very unlikely they could be thought of as conservative, but they were not dare-devils and if any of them thought they might die with an airplane strapped on their ass they never said so. Only Moravia mentioned the possibility once in a while and he was just trying to do his job.

He could remember only one pilot he had ever seen wearing a tie. That was Kalberer who was flying the mail back east somewhere for National Air Transport. But he had always been a fancy dresser. There was also Slim Lindbergh of course, who now wore a tie occasionally because he was so famous and had to meet a lot of important people. The rest of the crowd, the day-after-day guy who made his living flying the mails or just barnstorming around the country, usually did not own a tie.

He asked himself how he could think of such things when there were much more important demands on his brain.

Now there was no sound of snow ticking along the fuselage and the pilot knew it must be very deep. There was only an almost suffocating silence. Still, that was healthy. He did not like to think what it would be like on the mountain if there was much wind.

He was lying on a piece of fabric with a mail sack for a pillow, and he shifted position slightly just to hear the familiar squeaking of his leather jacket. At least it was some sound. Moments later he heard Heather's muffled voice. "Are you awake?"

"Yes, are you warm enough?" He didn't dare ask if she hurt.

"Oh, yes. I've been thinking. What's your name?"

"Jerry."

"*Mister* Jerry? My mom says I should call older people Mister or Missus."

"Just call me Jerry."

"I guess while I'm here it won't hurt to pretend I'm a grown-up."

"Why not? I'm beginning to think you are."

And that was sure the damn truth, he decided. In the darkness it was very difficult to envision Heather as a child.

They were silent for a long time and he hoped she had fallen asleep when he heard her again, and somehow her voice sounded even more frail. God almighty, he thought, she can't be dying. It's just her back.

"I have all the clothes," she was saying. "You must be cold."

"No. I've slept in this jacket a hundred times."

"What's the name of your wife?"

"I don't have one."

Another silence followed, then she asked, "Is she dead?"

"No. I never have had a wife."

"Why?"

Now there, he decided, was one question he did not feel obliged to answer. Even to a little girl on a mountain. How could he say, "Listen, little Heather. Maybe you failed to take a good look at me. How would you like to look at this face every morning and maybe all day long? And just how does a man get himself married in the first place? To meet wives you first had to meet girls and they were not to be found in the sky or, except for a very few, around airports. They were to be found in churches or dance halls, depending on what sort they were, or speakeasies, or social clubs, or some kind of place where people gathered together because they found each other's company made them feel better. Well, I tried it a few times, soon after the accident, and I saw what happened all right. People would shake my hand and try to smile and even try to make conversation. They would be looking all the time at the floor or the ceiling or anywhere except at me and they would find someone else to be with just as quickly as they could. It did not take long for me to understand what was happening and I could not really blame them. So in the interest of the general public's comfort I just decided not to depress them any more than I could help."

He cleared his throat as if he were giving Heather's question serious consideration and said, "I don't know why I never got married. I guess . . . until today, well, maybe I have been just too much in love with flying."

"At least it's good to be in love with *some*thing."

"You are very wise for your age."

"But . . . have you ever been really, *really* in love? With a real girl I mean?"

Now there again was something he did not care to discuss; at least with a stranger, and for the past eight years, that is almost ever since the accident, it seemed everyone was in the stranger class. And he had not been inclined to even think of Sally any more than he could help, much less discuss her. Yet now, because a stranger had asked a question she thought was innocent, here was Sally once more imposing on his thoughts.

It had been no use trying to deny that he had been totally in love with Sally, and regardless of the outcome he would not allow anything to damage the memories of the joyous times they had known together. After one weekend in San Antonio, Sally had said almost exactly the same words he had heard a few minutes ago. "You are a very beautiful man."

Yet now he knew the words were far from the same, because Sally had been looking directly in his face. He had been standing by the window of their hotel room, his body still warm and tingling from their love-making, and afterward they had talked for the first time about how much easier things would be if they were married.

They had agreed to "sometime in October."

Sally was still trying to choose a specific date when the accident occurred.

A month passed in the hospital before they told him the worst about the damages to his body and the ravages to his face. He was a tin-and-pin man and when at last he forced himself to look in a mirror he failed to recognize the artificial human he saw.

Sally had not run away from the calamity; she suggested they be married right in the hospital. But her eyes said so clearly, "I'm going through with this thing because it is the only decent thing to do."

Sally had been cheated. She deserved and wanted a whole man.

One more long look in the mirror made his decision relatively easy. A sudden change of mind, he had explained. "Sorry, Sally, I've had a chance to do a lot of thinking and now I don't think it would work for the two of us."

For Sally, running out on another's misfortune was unthinkable. So it had taken some extra doing to discourage her. For a while she came to the hospital regularly although the nurses cooperated in a "no visitors" policy.

Two months passed before Sally gave up and just disappeared. A buddy who was still flying for the Army volunteered she had gone to Chicago and married a reporter for the *Tribune*.

Now he said to the darkness, "Heather, how come a girl your age asks such questions? How old are you, anyway?"

"Eleven . . . going on twelve. You think I still play with dolls?"

"Well, I'm not much of an authority on the habits of young ladies because my life just hasn't worked out like most peoples'."

"I wish you would tell me about your life."

"Why, for gosh sake?"

"If I can listen to you about anything maybe then my back won't hurt so much because my brain won't be able to worry about two things at the same time. That's what my teacher keeps telling us in school. Don't be a flibbertigibbet. Don't be trying to think about a whole bunch of things all at once because it's bad for you . . . that is, she doesn't mean bad for your health or anything like that, but bad for passing tests and things like that. She says we have to learn to concentrate and if I can concentrate on you then I can't concentrate on my back if you see what I mean. Everyone has this problem. Flibbertigibbets are all over the world and not just here in America I think."

"I wish I could help you more," he said. "Would it feel better if I rolled you over on your side? . . . I would be very careful."

She hesitated. "I guess you'd better try because it seems to be getting worse."

Moving with extreme caution lest he bump her in the darkness he reached out until he found her shoulders and then moved his hand slowly down to her hip. "Let's just take it easy."

He eased his other hand slowly behind her neck, and told her to take a deep breath and exhale. Then he rolled her very gently toward him.

For an instant he thought all would be well. He felt her warm breath on his cheek and he thought with sudden pleasure that at this moment he was closer to Heather than he had been to another human being in eight years.

She caught her breath and a choked little cry escaped her.

"Oh no . . . *no!* Please let me down . . ."

He eased her back into her original position and waited in despair for her quick sobs to diminish.

"Just . . . stay there. Try to relax for tonight. We'll think of something in the morning."

"It hurts so. Even if I move a teeny bit—"

He reached out to her face and felt her tears. He brought out his handkerchief and wiped the tears away. He continued to caress her cheeks. "I don't like to give you another pill if you can stand to be without it."

"Why not?"

Why not, indeed? As he heard her catching at her

breath in jerky little whimpers he wondered if he dared tell her she might need the pills even more to-morrow. If help failed to come, if somehow by some supreme miraculous effort he could take her to help, then the pills might make it possible.

"They just might not be good for you . . . too many that is."

"I wish I could go to sleep . . ."

"You will. Will it hurt if I rub the back of your neck?"

"I don't think so." Her voice sounded so feeble that even in the stillness he could hardly hear her.

His fingers found the warmth of her neck and moved very gently in small circles. "Okay, Heather?"

"Yes . . . okay."

As his fingers moved and she quieted he began to talk to her in the darkness. He tried to keep his voice low and soothing and after a time he realized the tense-ness was leaving her and she was breathing regularly.

It had been so long since he had talked at length with another human he now found it awkward to begin. There was so much he longed to share, his thoughts seemed to meet each other head on.

"I guess there really isn't much to tell about my life, Heather . . . I was born and then I grew for a while and I made friends along the way. Some of them I still hear from once in a while, but people change and we drift away and since I've been flying the people I went to school with don't seem to talk the same language. I have one friend now who is very special . . . although I suppose he doesn't consider me really a friend. His name is Moravia and he is my boss and it is very diffi-cult to explain how I really feel about him. He has only one leg and maybe that made it easier for him to hire me, but I can tell you right now without any trouble at all that the day he interviewed me and said that I had the job . . . well, I just can't tell you what that did for me. I had been to every flying outfit I could find in this country and they all looked at me like I was a ghost and told me how lucky I was to be alive. They offered me ground jobs but no one wanted me to fly for them. Moravia was not spooked by the way I looked and when you meet people like that you just want to hold on to them and do your best for them. He is a strange man, Moravia . . . the more I know him the less I know him . . ."

The pilot had no conception of how long he talked. He slipped into a near trance as he told her of his early flying days. He told her how his parents had taken him to the Nebraska State Fair where he had seen a small yellow airplane fly. Looking up, his mouth wide in fascination, he could see the sunlight through the wings and on the bottom wing and also the top where the pilot had his name painted for everyone to see . . . *Beechy*. He had thought the little flying machine was the most beautiful thing he had ever seen and he vowed right then and there that he would one day fly himself.

. . . Later there was a man named Sloniger who had taught him to fly a "Jennie" he had bought right after the war. Sloniger flew the mail with Lindbergh before he became so famous, and he was still flying somewhere back east.

". . . There was the usual thing, the barnstorming all over the country, north with the sun in the summer and south with the birds in winter . . . a gypsy life, Heather, without much point to it. Then the army needed instructors in primary flight training and the job was regular and paid well . . . and they employed civilians when they could find them reliable and sober during the day."

He realized at last that he was talking to himself, for the girl's breathing had become almost regular and she had been silent for a long time.

He lowered his head until he could feel her breath on the good side of his face and he thought that if ever he had wanted anything in the world it would be to kiss her cheek which was incredibly soft and smooth.

He withdrew his hand very slowly from the back of her neck and waited. Finally he whispered, "Thank you, little girl."

He bent down until his twisted mouth almost touched her cheek and all the yearning for affection he had known for eight long years rose to help him form his lips into a gentle kiss.

He retreated almost instantly as if he had done something very wrong.

MORAVIA was upset with himself because he had chosen to sleep in his office. What an unforgivable, sentimental gesture! There was absolutely nothing he could do during the night and every available contact had reported to him before darkness fell.

They were all discouraging. Elko: —Fourteen had taken off almost two hours behind schedule. He had not returned, nor had Elko had any positive response from those few people they had managed to contact along the route.

Boise the same. Fourteen had never appeared there and so it was reasonable to assume that he had landed somewhere in between Boise and Elko. Yet Moravia's rancher near Rome, who had finally answered his telephone, said that if Fourteen had landed right in his back pasture he would not have been able to see him. It was snowing that heavily.

Did he take to his chute and somehow haul the girl along with him? Of course not. No pilot with an ounce of sanity would leave the relative protection of his aircraft and risk a parachute landing in the middle of nowhere. Not if he had enough light to land his airplane.

All sheriffs and forest rangers and such police as

there were along the line had been alerted to the possibility of a downed aircraft, and Moravia had badgered the weather bureaus in both Salt Lake and San Francisco trying to obtain a definite prognosis on the weather. His dissatisfaction mounted as he listened to a long series of "hems and haws" and "ifs" and practiced equivocations. No one in the U.S. Weather Bureaus was going to be caught with sunshine pouring on the landscape when they said it would be snowing. "If they would only look out the window," Moravia sighed.

Now as he drank the stale coffee in the waiting room and sucked on his first Caporal of the day, he repented his night on the couch. At home he always removed his artificial limb and, thus relieved, slept reasonably well. Now his stump was irritated and his outlook on the grey dawn was a match. If he had gone home Marsha would have soothed him and he might have had a good night's rest instead of fretting helplessly over Fourteen's fate. He cursed his imagination.

Fourteen could have encountered ice and failed to get himself out of it immediately. He could have postponed his decision to follow the old airman's dictum . . . that a 180-degree turn is the safest maneuver in the business. As few as two minutes in clear ice and his airplane might become uncontrollable.

Fourteen could have climbed on top of an overcast rather than hunt through the valleys like a ferret, and once above the clouds found too late that the holes he expected were just not there. With nothing to guide him over a vast sea of white except his rather dicey magnetic compass he could become lost. As his fuel reserve slipped away with the minutes he would have to descend through the cloud into the unknown. Then Fourteen would sweat in spite of the cold for he would know that within that cloud layer might be granite. Moravia could picture such a predicament all too easily. He had been there.

He considered the possibility of engine failure in flight and dismissed it as not worth adding to his real fears. Engines did sometimes fail under the pressure of full take-off power, but trouble at cruise was extremely rare.

Long after dusk and well into the night, Moravia told himself that soon enough his phone would ring and it would be Fourteen reporting himself as having set down in some pleasant field, albeit far from a telephone. The weather, of course; Fourteen was a laconic man and would not elaborate except to say that the mail was safe and he would be off as soon as the local conditions cleared.

Yet as the hours passed Moravia lost ever more faith in his analysis. The sharp remarks he had formed in his mind about Fourteen's taking his goddamned time about reporting gradually soured.

Fourteen was no careless fool. He knew people would be concerned about him and he was an extremely sensitive man. He was the only pilot Moravia had ever known who had three books of poetry in what passed for his home, and last October when a symphony played in Salt Lake he had asked for an extra day off so he could attend. Fourteen was not one to land in some farmer's field, accept a congratulatory series of drinks and, as Moravia knew only too well had actually happened, forget where he came from and where he was going.

Nor was Fourteen likely to have a girl friend living along the route, who might tempt him to land for a fast hello. That sort of thing had also happened.

As the hours passed and midnight came with no report from anywhere or anyone, Moravia knew that Fourteen must be in serious trouble—if indeed he was alive. The fact that he was carrying a passenger as well as the mail only made it more vexatious and complicated.

Moravia was haunted by the faces of the girl's grandparents. They had come in all innocence to meet the airplane, arriving well ahead of the appointed one o'clock. Then as the afternoon passed and nothing came out of the sky, he had at last told them that it was unlikely anything would be coming. When they had extracted the last iota of hope from him and he could no longer postpone the truth, they had collapsed on his office couch and refused to leave until long after dark.

Even more difficult was his obligatory call to the girl's parents, who lived near Elko. At least, he thought, he was spared the sight of their faces as he told them there was an excellent chance the pilot would be calling in soon, and since he was so skillful their daughter would doubtless regard the whole thing as no more than an exciting adventure. The parents sounded very intelligent and seemed to remain calm although they did say they hoped he was not lying. "I am not cruel," he had responded rather testily in his anxiety. "And I am an optimist."

Finally he had thought to call on Fourteen's behalf. But who? After some searching he found Fourteen's original application in the office file, a formality he had completed after he had actually been hired. He had designated both parents as deceased. There was a box at the bottom of the page marked "Notify in case of accident: Next of kin or friends."

The box was empty.

He called the agent who handled the company employee insurance, hoping Fourteen would have named a beneficiary. The agent said the spacing provided for such names had not been filled in.

Empty like his life, Moravia thought. He had known his kind before. For one reason or another, usually never revealed, they had turned their backs on the human race and when they died they just died.

Now with the dawn there was much to do. He could stop scratching at his stubble of beard and get on the telephone. By ten he would have three pilots and their airplanes searching the northern section of the route where the weather was still passable if not ideal. The National Guard had promised the assistance of all their available aircraft, but it would be afternoon before they arrived from Spokane. And at eleven, willy-nilly, there would be the southbound mail to be flown.

Moravia was grateful there were still so many things to be done. They would ease the gradual decay in his belief that Fourteen would soon be found.

AT first the pilot thought it was the wind which had come with the dawn and caused an intermittent flapping somewhere along the side of the shelter. Then, as he awakened more fully, he realized the faint keening sound came from the girl. It was a high-pitched, plaintive lament that followed the cadence of her breathing. The pilot wondered how long he could stand to hear it.

"Are you awake?" he asked finally.

"Yes." There was only silence after her one word. He hoped she would go back to sleep, but the keening sound persisted.

He waited as long as he could, then he asked, "How goes it?"

He wondered if she had heard him since she made no reply. "Today will be a big day," he said. "We'll get out of here somehow. What would you like for breakfast? The management regrets to inform you that we are out of both cereal and bananas. And I'll be darned if we aren't just fresh out of both bacon and eggs and the cook burned the last piece of toast . . . so will you settle for a nice chunk of chocolate bar?"

"Yes." He thought her voice was very faint.

"How do you want it? Sunny-side up or over? If you can wait a little bit I'll build a fire outside and make you some pine-needle tea. They say it will cure anything."

"My back . . . could I have a pill now?"

"Sure." He shook a pill from the little bottle and crawled to the entrance. He reached outside, gathered a handful of snow, and carefully placed the pill in the center. He made a miniature snowball and crawled back to Heather. "Here. Pretend it is ice cream."

Still on his knees he looked down at her as she swallowed.

"Good morning," he said. He saw her try to smile, but the expression was far different from the one he had seen before. "Did anyone ever tell you that you are a very pretty girl in the morning?"

He saw a strange concern in her eyes. Suddenly he realized that because of the shelter's low ceiling he was bent over her, his face hardly more than a foot from hers. And now bright daylight filtered through the parachute silk.

He retreated instantly, backing away crab-fashion, horrified that the vision of his face hovering so closely over her might have shocked her. "I'll go out now and make a fire. We'll have some good hot tea to cheer us up."

He crawled quickly out of the shelter and stood up. A fitful, bitter wind struck his cheeks and the same wind picked up little plumes of snow and sent them twirling down the mountain.

He looked up at the close-packed clouds and saw they were moving rapidly. We are on the lee side and for damn sure we are very lucky, he thought. And there will be sun today.

The balance of what he beheld depressed him. The snow had obliterated the trench dug by the fuselage and it was obvious that finding enough wood for a fire was going to take a long time. It was much clearer below and he thought that he had been better off when he had been spared the view. Now he saw that he had landed on a wide plateau which was littered with enormous boulders along the higher perimeter. The bottom edge was equally uninviting. There appeared to be an almost vertical drop-off into a frozen valley far below. Escape or access via that route seemed to be impossible.

He made himself count the good things. The plateau was sheltered from the present winds, and the trees might offer some protection if the wind swung to the south. And they were not cramped for room. He could walk in either direction as far as he could see as long as he stayed at approximately the same level as the shelter.

He trudged off through the knee-deep snow in search of wood.

THE sun had risen by the time he had gathered an armful of broken branches from the area where the Stearman's wings had torn through the trees. The wood was green and heavy with sap and he knew it would not make much of a fire. He worried about an errant spark setting fire to the shelter, so he dug a hole in the snow some distance from it. Then he cut shavings from the branches which he remembered he had not done since his days as a Boy Scout, stacked them carefully in the hole and finally, after using four of his precious matches, had a fire which promised to keep burning.

He decided that as soon as he had given Heather tea he would try to drain the oil from the engine, construct some kind of container, and soak the branches in it. Maybe then he would have a real fire.

He was proud of his two cooking utensils. They were the cone-like housings which contained the Stearman's landing lights. One was badly crumpled, but it stood by itself better than the other and he used it now to make water. He was shocked by how much snow he had to feed into his crude bucket to make even a half-inch of water in the bottom.

He blessed the tool kit which had enabled him to remove two of the engine's rocker arm covers. They would serve as shallow cups and he had carefully scrubbed them with snow to remove the sludge of oil. And who knew? Perhaps the remaining aroma of oil might complement pine needles. Perhaps the engine which had proven so false might become their salvation.

The fire made snapping sounds which he found reassuring, but the continuous feeding of snow to make so little water was discouraging. And several times the capricious wind alternated between enveloping him in smoke and bringing to him the disturbing sounds from the shelter. He could hear Heather's low moaning and he wondered how long he could bear it at close range.

He looked at the sun which clipped in and out of the clouds as if reflecting his spirits, and he told the smoke and the mountain and the clouds that he was not a religious man and was not asking for help for himself, but would God, if he was awake, please help a nice little girl who probably would also be clumsy about asking for his assistance.

"Something has to stop her from making those noises," he muttered aloud. "Something . . . somehow . . . I can't stand it much longer and neither can she. Something has to be done to distract—"

Then he thought that if he was talking to himself after less than one day on the mountain they were already slipping into worse trouble.

He forced himself to think about what he must do this day. First, the fire—keep it going. Take oil from the engine and put it in some kind of receptacle made out of something. Keep handy near the fire to make black smoke in case he heard an airplane engine.

Next, food. In another hour or two they were going to know what it was like to be really hungry.

Where had he put his mail gun, the silly blunderbuss with the holster so shiny from rubbing against his hip?

Never fired. As he remembered, it held six shells or was it eight? He wondered if a man who had shot a pistol only once before in his life could hit anything more than a few feet away.

But where was the gun? While he raked his confused memories of the day before, his hand reached instinctively for his hip. What have you done with the gun, *fat*-head? It could make the difference between you and the girl surviving and not suriviving.

He stood up quickly, his thoughts hammering at his inadequacies. Jesus H. Christ, can't you ever do *any*thing right? You land with a perfectly good gun and lose it first thing. It isn't the little girl who needs a nurse . . . it's you!

Then suddenly he hoped he knew. He left the fire and ran through the snow to the shelter. He halted within a few steps of the Stearman's snow-covered tail and approached it warily. If the gun was not where he supposed, he would search within the shelter even though he knew it was not there. Because the gun had to be somewhere, and the idea that because of his lack of foresight it might be buried just anywhere beneath the snow was just more than he could tolerate right at this damn start of the day.

A man who had his wits about him would of course have been careful to stash the gun in some very safe place first thing. He would know exactly where it was and by this time would already have something ready for the pot. No doubt about it, a squirrel, or a goat, or a bear maybe, or whatever the hell lived on the side of a mountain. And died there, besides people.

A man should know about such things, he thought, and all you know is how to fly an airplane. And there was now considerable evidence strewn around this mountain that maybe testified you were not so very good at that.

Finding a gun in this snow would be sheer luck—unless it was where it was supposed to be.

The sound of the girl's whimpering forced him to move.

He pushed his hand slowly through the snow along the top of the fuselage. He advanced his feet a step at a time, exploring tenderly lest he push the gun off into deeper snow and maybe never find it again. It is here, he thought, right here—somewhere. Now his whole world seemed centered on this one object which he had so long treated with contempt. He held his breath in his anxiety.

The snow piled up to his elbow and slid away as his hand uncovered inch after inch of the Stearman's pale grey fabric. Because the fuselage lay on its left side his plowing revealed a part of the letters U.S. Soon, he knew, there would be part of the letter M and then A and then the rest of the word MAIL. And somewhere along here he was positive he had placed the gun. Well, fairly sure.

He stopped his hand as his fingers encountered something solid. He held his breath as he allowed his cold fingers to rise slightly beneath the snow and continue forward until his hand covered the object. Then suddenly he clutched it with all his strength, pulled his hand away in a flurry of snow and said aloud, "There you are, you bastard."

He brought the gun and holster to his lips and kissed it. And he thought, I am going mad. Kissing guns in the morning!

From beneath the snow he heard her call his name. "Jerry?"

Still clutching the gun he dropped to his knees and crawled inside the shelter. Although Heather's mouth was strained he persuaded himself that some of the sparkle he remembered had returned to her eyes.

She said, "I heard you talking to someone. Have they come for us already?"

"No. I was just talking with myself. I hope it doesn't become a habit."

"I talk to myself all the time. All my friends do."

She watched him place the gun very carefully under the mail sack he had been using as a pillow. "What are you going to do with that gun?"

"Nothing, probably. I just had an idea it might come in handy in case I wanted to shoot something."

"Why would you want to shoot anything? You're such a nice person and I just can't imagine any animal not liking you a whole lot."

"Well, I like animals too, but—"

He tried not to appear furtive as he tucked the gun under the mail sack. There, now he knew exactly where it was. "If you're thinking of killing some animals for food, well, I'm not hungry," she said.

He detected a note of peevishness in her voice and he thought that was a hopeful sign. Somewhere he had heard, maybe his mother had told him when he was sick as a boy, that people always became peevish when they were on the way to recovery. He cautioned himself not to tell her there might soon come a time when she would be hungry.

"How does your back feel?" he asked.

"It still hurts. Can I have another pill?"

"No. It's too soon."

"It doesn't feel too soon. I have never hurt so much." She was silent for a moment, then she asked, "When do you think they will come?"

"Maybe today . . . maybe not until tomorrow."

"Are you sure?"

If I begin to lie now, he thought, then I will have to start a whole series of lies and sooner or later get trapped. Then she will not believe whatever it is I'll have to tell her when that time comes . . . when things get really tough—

"No. I'm not sure when they will come," he said as he adjusted the teddy bear around her legs. Trying to dismiss the doubts, he said that her tea was almost ready and he would bring it soon. And he found while

64

he fussed with the flight suit that he could not bear to look into her eyes. Deliberately mumbling his words, as if his present care was part of a long-established routine between them, he asked if she wanted to go to the bathroom or anything like that, and when she declined he warned her not to hesitate calling on him for anything. ". . . Just any old thing and I'm at your service."

Then, still without meeting her eyes, he crawled out of the shelter and stood watching the vapor of his breath blow away on the wind.

When he heard the whimpering start again he went down to the fire where he could not hear it.

STILLER, one of the oldest pilots of the line, was not happy with the morning because the overcast was low and sliding across the dreary Nevada landscape at a pace that told him of strong winds aloft. For sure he would have a bumpy ride with the northbound mail out of Elko and probably a continuous wrestling match with his airplane over the more mountainous areas. Worse, he would have to stay just under the overcast, thereby limiting his altitude and field of vision. For on the flight north he had been told to keep a sharp eye on the terrain. One of the line's airplanes was down somewhere along the route—that fellow Jerry whom no one seemed to know very well. Stiller was not surprised that on this morning he could not even remember Jerry's last name.

Never mind. He *was* peculiar and certainly a loner, but he had twice volunteered to take Stiller's flight when he had wanted to spend an extra day with the family. With five children you appreciated a man making gestures like that and certainly Jerry had known enough tough luck in his life.

Probosky, the mechanic, held the parachute straps as he slipped into it. Some pilots put it on in the airplane and saved an awkward walk with the chute banging against the back of their thighs, but Stiller liked to be assured his could serve as more than a seat cushion. He wanted to have a good look at the D-ring assembly rather than just a glance at it. With five kids you thought that way.

When he clipped the shoulder straps together and then brought up the leg straps, he straightened and fastened the chin strap of his helmet. And he swore for the hundredth time that when he got to Pasco he was not going to just hurry home as he usually did. He was going to stop by the repair hangar, find a leather punch, and put a new hole in the chin strap. As it was and had been for more than a year of forgetting to make the alteration, the holes were in the wrong place. Using hole number one made the helmet too loose and the next brought up the chin strap until it nearly choked him. Cutting a new hole with a knife was risky business because the chin strap was built into the helmet. You could ruin the whole helmet that way and for a family man they were expensive.

If you were a family man you counted your pennies so there would be a few left at the end of the month. Caution was the word at all times. Caution in flight led to long life. Caution . . . always caution.

Stiller was pleased with his thinking. He had convinced himself that his prudent philosophy was responsible for twelve years of flying without scratching an airplane or himself.

MORAVIA thought it had been one of the longest days he had ever known. He was slumped in the leather chair behind his desk sucking occasionally on a Caporal and rubbing more frequently at his sore eyes. He was disgusted. A shaft of late afternoon sunlight angled down from the high office window and illuminated Stiller who sat opposite him. His teddy bear was unbuttoned and his white scarf hung loosely about his neck. For a moment the light made him appear almost luminescent, a phenomenon lost on Moravia. He watched Stiller toy with the chin strap of his helmet and he thought it was unforgivable for the man to seem so relaxed, considering the circumstances.

Moravia glared at him. "Do you mean to sit there and tell me that you actually saw a wing and what looked like pieces of a fuselage and you didn't go down to confirm it?"

"You don't understand. I just had a peek down through a hole. And not a very big hole."

"Well, why the hell didn't you dive down through the hole and have a better look?"

"There was a lot of wind. It was rougher than a cob. Near the side of a mountain like that I might have hit some heavy down-drafts and never been able to climb out. Then you would have had two airplanes to look for."

"That's a chance I might be willing to take in exchange for confirmation," Moravia muttered. Mother of God, why did it have to be this chicken-hearted son-of-a-bitch who just thought he might have seen something? All the other pilots who had been aloft this day, and who would certainly have gone down through any hole had there been one available, had reported no sighting of anything even remotely interesting.

He studied Stiller's thin lips and bland expression and decided again that he had never liked the man's sanctimonious air. Then he tried to bury his frustration along with his temper.

"Let me get this straight," he began as easily as he could manage. "You took off from Elko and ran into more wind than you expected. You were off course to the west maybe twenty or thirty miles and on top of a broken overcast. You were not exactly sure where you were until you realized by what you saw below that you were over more mountainous terrain than you should be. Is that essentially correct?"

"Essentially . . . yes. I knew there would be wind, but not that much."

"Okay. Now you just happened to be looking down when you saw a hole with a wing and a fuselage at the bottom of it—"

"I *think* that's what I saw."

"Well, goddamn it, you know what a wing and fuselage looks like. Was it or wasn't it?"

"From that altitude it was hard to be sure. And the whole side of the mountain was covered with heavy snow. So was whatever it was I saw. You can't imagine how small it was."

"I can imagine. From the altitude you were flying things are bound to look small." Moravia found it impossible to keep the sarcasm from his voice. "I suppose it never occurred to you to descend?"

"Yes, it did. I even turned around and went back over the area, but the hole was gone. I circled around above the overcast for about five minutes before I gave up."

"Five minutes," Moravia said flatly.

"With the way the wind was blowing I had to think of my fuel. It occurred to me that if it swung around to the north I might not make Boise."

And it could be, Moravia thought, that you left a buddy to die right under you. It could be that if you had just waited a little longer there might have been another hole and you could dive down and have a look around and still have more than enough fuel remaining to get you to a nice flat field for an emergency landing. And the hell with any delay of the mail.

Yet Moravia kept his recriminations to himself and laid his palm over the map beneath his desk glass. "So far as you know you were somewhere in this area . . . over the Santa Rosa range in Nevada?"

Stiller leaned forward to better view the map. "I'm

quite sure I was more to the northeast. I'm reasonably sure I saw Capitol Peak sticking up through the overcast."

Moravia grunted and he made no attempt to hide his bitterness. "That would put whatever you thought you saw somewhere up here in the wilderness, which only leaves us a mere few thousand square miles to search."

"If you're through with me," Stiller said anxiously, "I'd just as soon get on home." He tried to smile. "My wife has a lot of things she wants me to do."

Moravia lit a Caporal from the butt of the one he was smoking. "Sure," he said. "Just stay near the telephone. I may need you."

As Stiller rose and shuffled through the door in his heavy boots, Moravia noted the special stoop in his posture. And he could not decide whether Stiller was a man simply burdened with domestication or a man who knew he had failed not only a comrade, but himself.

THE pilot could not believe the sun was already so low. All day he had reminded himself that if he lost his sense of humor entirely, then he must certainly lose the challenge which was becoming increasingly apparent. And he thought that he might die of many things on the mountain, but it would not be from boredom, for never had he been so busy.

The fire had gone out twice. Rekindling it and tending it, he now calculated, had taken him at least three hours. He had drained some oil from the engine, catching it as he had the girl's elimination in one of the wheel flanges. He experimented by pouring a little oil on the fire and producing a black smoke.

Twice during the late morning, he was convinced he had heard an airplane, but the wind was blowing hard enough to confuse all sounds. Later he decided it might have been just wishful thinking.

Ernest K. Gann

He had cut most of the fabric off the wings and some from the fuselage. He laid the pieces on the snow in such a way they formed a huge X. He secured the edges with chunks of shale. If there was no more snow then the X should be easily visible, he thought, although for better visibility he wished the Stearman had been painted any other color except neutral grey.

By the time he had finished with his chores, as he now thought of any activity, and had spent as much time as he could bear with Heather, it was mid-afternoon.

It was not easy, he kept reminding himself, to maintain a sense of humor when a little girl was hurting. He called himself a coward for giving her another pill and sneaking off under the pose of hunting.

Hail the mighty hunter! He had waded through the snow for two exhausting hours, skinned his knee on a rock when he had stepped into an invisible crevasse and frightened himself badly when he had slipped again and nearly gone over a high cliff.

When he first left the vicinity of the wreckage he found himself holding the gun almost at the ready as if, he thought, some rabbit or deer or antelope was determined to jump right out in front of him and commit suicide. Or an alligator perhaps? All during that early and mid-afternoon he had not seen a living creature. Worse, he had not even seen any tracks that a possible meal might have made. At best, he thought, continued stumbling around through and over unseen obstacles could result in his shooting himself in the foot.

His shadow was very long when he returned to the shelter. There he broke the remainder of the chocolate bar in several pieces and gave Heather one. He took only pine-needle tea for himself.

When she had finished the chocolate Heather began whimpering again and he thought that from now on he would have to start thinking of her as just "the girl." The name Heather was too personal and beautiful. It identified her as something he valued, someone he might even love perhaps, if he were given decent social time instead of this perpetual agony. When he had lain so long in the hospital, his body so battered the nurses thought he could never be put back together again, they never referred to him by name. They spoke of him only as "the aviator," thereby avoiding any personal involvement with his dubious future. Now, he thought, "the girl" must be stripped of her exactness. She must become any little girl and therefore her hurting might not find so much sympathy in his own body.

"If I am to keep my sanity," he resolved, "I cannot think of her as the dear friend she is becoming. I have to sterilize her. I have to force her to keep her distance or we'll go down the drain together. I cannot think or function efficiently if I have to suffer right along with her."

Things had to change. Otherwise his tolerance was going to break down. He might even shout, "Will you for Christ's sake stop that whining?" As he longed to do.

Yet he must not weaken, he must cut off even a trace of impatience within himself.

She whimpered again and he hoped he could keep his vow. "Is there anything I can do to make you more comfortable?"

There was not the honest solicitude in his voice he would have liked to have heard. The tone reminded him somewhat of Sally's voice during her visits to the hospital in San Antonio. There were times when no matter what she said it sounded like she was pleading with him to stop his loafing in bed, to rise up, and get going.

Now he noticed with some annoyance that Heather had not responded to his concern.

"I asked you a question. Cat got your tongue?"

Still, she said nothing. He waited, listening to the almost inaudible whirring of the wind through the tree-

71

tops. "It's going to be dark pretty soon and if there's anything I can do for you, then it will be much easier to do it now."

At last he heard her whisper, "I hurt so . . ."

Was she coming right out with it and blaming him for her pain? How many hundred times did she have to say she hurt? Look, you silly little girl, *I* did not make the damned engine so don't be blaming me.

"If I give you another pill now then we'll be all out of pills by sometime tomorrow and we just might need them for . . . something."

"I need them now."

"Well, for Chri—!" He caught himself. "Tell you what I'll do. We'll take a chance. I think I got all the fuel out of the tank so I'll bring the fire in here to sort of cheer things up. How would you like that?"

"It would be nice."

He scrambled out the entrance. It was getting easier every time, he thought, like a rat zipping in and out of its hole. A human being could adapt himself to anything . . . almost. That is, if he kept his sense of humor.

There were two good embers left in the little fire pit and he brought them to the shelter. There near the entrance, he dug a shallow pit. He cut off some shavings from the best piece of wood he had been able to find and fed them carefully to the embers. In time he created a bright little fire, but the smoke was heavy.

"The smoke is getting in my eyes," Heather said.

"Well, I can't stop it."

Where there was smoke there was fire, for the love of God! Should he tell her this was where all those phrases originated, like "you can't have your cake and eat it too"? And where did she get off complaining—considering the situation?

"Do you want me to take the fire outside again?"

He thought he would be damned if he would even if she asked him. Sure it was smoky in the shelter, his own eyes were watering, but wasn't fire man's first and best friend? "Did you know that?" he asked, while he wondered what was happening to his mind that he should be thinking of such things.

"Know what?"

Why did he have to be stuck on a mountain with a dumb little girl who could not even carry on an intelligent conversation? Well, that was the story of his life all right . . . all right. You did things for people and they barely bothered to thank you.

"I asked you if you knew that fire was man's first and best friend."

"You never asked me that."

"I didn't? Well, let's not make a federal case out of it."

"Federal case? What are you talking about?"

"That's just a phrase people use when they want to call a halt to a disagreement . . . or argument, or— well, it means let's not make so much of this thing that a high federal court has to decide who was right."

"Please don't talk down to me, Jerry. *Please.*"

Crim*inee!* What was happening here? "Okay, okay, o*kay,*" he heard himself saying. And for the life of me, he thought, I cannot get that note of annoyance out of my voice. "I apologize."

"You don't have to apologize for anything, Jerry."

"Yes, I do." And do I ever, he thought. "Let's get back on the original track. Is there anything I can do for you before it gets dark, which from the looks of things outside won't be long?"

"You could tell me some more about your life so I could concentrate on that instead of my back."

"There's nothing more to tell you." There was a hell of a lot more, he thought, but who could make sense out of it to a dumb little girl?

Suddenly he was inspired. Hey! The notion spun down out of the smoke and asked for action. Hey! Why not? At last here was something that might be a distraction.

73

He reached across the shelter to the mail sack he had been using as a pillow. He pulled it to him, untied the draw strings, and took out a handful of letters. Arranging five letters in his hand like cards he offered them to Heather. "Pick any one," he said. "We'll open it and see what the writer has to say."

She hesitated. "Won't that be prying into other people's business?"

"Not if we promise not to look at the addresses of the sender. And whoever they are they'll never know the difference anyway. In this situation I would say it's permissible."

And very necessary, he thought. Here was something that might get the girl's mind on something besides her back. "Go ahead. Pick one," he urged.

She closed her eyes a moment as if to guarantee her selection would be chance, then pulled one letter from his hand. He took out his knife and slit it open for her.

"You want me to read it to you?" she asked.

He nodded and waited for her to commence. He thought that he did not give a damn what the letter said if it kept Heather—no, *the girl*—busy and his mind off their troubles. Terrible things could happen around here in a few days unless he found something—

He waited and still she remained silent. In the gloom he could see she was reading the letter, but she seemed reluctant to share it with him. While only minutes before he had yearned for her to be quiet now he found her silence strangely annoying.

"Are you going to read it or not?" He allowed his impatience to creep into his voice again and decided he did not care.

"Well . . . ?" he intoned.

"This is sort of a funny letter, that is, it is not really funny like the Katzenjammer Kids or something like that. It is really sad and I'm not sure I understand what the person is trying to say."

"In about five minutes we are going to be in the dark

and you won't be reading anything. So you better hurry up." He placed a twig on the fire and tried not to ignore the ache of hunger in his belly. Maybe he could make some kind of a trap from parts of the wreckage and set it just outside? There it would be all night and then breakfast would be waiting in the morning.

"This letter is from a lawyer and this is what it says. 'Dear Mister Antonivich: We are pleased to report that we have finally made a settlement out of court with the Nevada Mining Corporation with respect to your injuries sustained in March of 1926. The settlement is for a sum of one thousand dollars and in accordance with our previous agreement the check was made out in our name . . .'"

She paused and said, "There is a word here I don't understand. Co–in–cidental–ly?"

"Coincidentally, maybe?"

Satisfied she read on. "'. . . We have retained these monies for our own account since *coincidentally* the amount happens to match our fee for attorney's services rendered in this matter. May we take this opportunity to wish you continued recovery. Kindest regards,' and it's signed by a Mister J. K. Monroe."

She handed the letter to the pilot and puckered her nose. "I don't think I like Mr. Monroe."

He put the letter in the envelope and stuffed it back in the sack. He wanted to say that he liked Mr. Monroe because he had obviously caused the girl to think about something other than her own troubles.

He slit open another letter and handed it to her. "Try this one."

"It's pretty hard to read, but I'll try. The handwriting is not Palmer method like we learn in school. It looks like it is written by my friend Roger who sits behind me and broke his arm and tried to write a composition with it in a sling and even the teacher couldn't read it. This one says, 'Dear Mom: I guess you have not heard from me since Pop died and maybe it was some time

75

before that. So I'm saying I'll spend the extra money and write you a letter air mail. Well I guess I'm sorry Pop did die even though he never sent me no money to speak of. Now I wonder if maybe the old man had a change of heart and maybe left me some dollars in his will. Even though we never got along too good I guess blood is thicker than water. Ha! Ha! So if there is any money just send it right away to this here address below. Of course if you and Sister swallowed *all* the loot I hope it rots in your pockets because that is not fair. Okay. I guess everything is all right with you two because I hear no different. Your son, Carl.' "

The pilot tried to smile. And for that sort of thing, he thought, I sometimes risk the only life I have.

She asked him to explain the letters to her and he made a halfhearted attempt. But he could find no logical way to explain cunning to a young girl who he was beginning to think must be lying about her age, and he had even less success with greed. By the time he had tried and his words faltered with confusion the only light in the shelter was a dim glow from the fire. "We had better try to sleep now," he said grumpily because he was dissatisfied with his inability to define the baser urgings of human behavior. "Do you want to go to the bathroom first?"

There was no response from beneath the pile of his teddy bear. Soon he suspected that he had said the wrong thing. The girl was crying again and her attempts to muffle her sobs seemed to make them all the more aggravating. Damn it, was he going to have to watch every word he said?

"Cut it out, Heather," he said before he could stop himself. Then to his amazement he heard himself adding, "Just please knock off the bawling, will you?"

If I bite my tongue off, he thought, our little world may spin more slowly. But holy simoleans, how could anyone be expected to keep a civil tongue in their heads when they were locked up in a cave about six feet long and four feet wide and three feet high? Right here was a bits-and-pieces grave occupied by a kid who was whining and a broken-down aviator who could not think what the hell to do to save his passenger, not to mention himself. Some hero.

"I'm sorry, Heather," he said. "I guess I'm getting sort of tired. Go ahead and cry all you want. I don't mind. Just tell me if you want to go to the bathroom and I'll get the bedpan."

He heard her say, "I am so embarrassed—"

Then he crawled to the entrance and reached out to retrieve the wheel flange which he had stuck edge-up in the snow. He brought it to the fire, warmed it to match the temperature of his hands, then moved on his hands and knees to Heather. "Here we are," he said softly as he lifted the folds of the teddy bear.

"Be brave now," he said as his hands sought her legs and lifted them very slowly until her knees were bent. She caught her breath several times but she did not cry out and he said, "Maybe you're getting better. Just relax as much as you can."

He eased one hand beneath her buttocks and raised her just enough to slip the flange beneath her. She groaned. Too much like an old woman, he thought, but she made no further sound and soon he heard the faint trickle of liquid he had been waiting for.

Because he was acutely aware that she was holding her breath he removed the flange too hastily and spilled urine on his hands and on the fabric where he slept. He smothered his regret in a desperate attempt to mentally redesign the flange; it was for damn sure too shallow for its present use.

He placed the flange behind him, then crawled to the entrance backward, pulling the flange after him. Once outside he stood up, emptied the flange, and washed it in the snow.

He looked up at the sky. A few snowflakes touched his face and he thought, This must be our last night on this mountain. Somehow I've got to find a way to get us out of this. As if the night might give him comfort he stood outside the shelter staring into the black void below. The only sound was the soft rustle of the parachute silk in the breeze.

He considered his few options, but he was lightheaded from hunger and he had difficulty separating wish from reality.

He could wait for someone to come, yet in the lives of the girl and himself that could be forever.

He could leave the girl here and try to make his way down the mountain by himself. That, of course, would be what he could have done if he had been alone, even though it would be in violation of the old rule to stay with a downed aircraft. A piece of wreckage was much easier to see from aloft than a human being.

He dismissed the idea almost instantly. He could not even consider leaving the girl for more than a few hours.

He raked his thoughts for other ways of escape and found only a now familiar one. They must go down the mountain together.

He looked down into the darkness and tried to imagine how many days it would take for a descent. Early in the day he had consulted the road map which served all mail pilots when they bothered to look at it. Spreading his fingers he had measured the approximate distance from where he thought he was to the little town of McDermitt. Most of the distance was along the mountain which was at least downhill. The last ten miles should be easier because from the look of the map they would be in a relatively flat valley. Still, the snow might be deeper there.

Time was wasting along with his strength. If he could find some way to carry Heather, then how long could he expect his strength to meet the demands of twenty-plus miles through the snow? She was a little girl, but she would become very heavy after a few hours.

Another unknown. What were the odds on leaving the protection of a shelter which might keep them alive for another week and taking a gamble on an open mountain? If the weather worsened or if he even slipped and fell, it would probably be death for both of them.

Suddenly he heard a scream behind him. The scream became a long, hysterical wail as he ran for the shelter. He scrambled quickly to Heather's side and found her trembling. She was almost incoherent.

"Please . . . *please* . . . Jerry . . . please help me!"

Her screaming mixed with wild sobbing as he took her in his arms. He heard her say something about a gun and then a long series of unintelligible mewings and cryings and finally, very clearly, he heard her say, "Please, Jerry . . . please kill me now . . . I can't stand it . . . please!"

He covered her mouth with his hand and wiped at her tears and tried to calm her flailing arms. As soon as he could manage he took the little bottle from his pocket, shook out a pill, and put it on her tongue. Then quickly he scraped up a chunk of snow from the corner of the shelter and pressed it after the pill.

He had no idea how long it was before she was quiet again because he tried desperately to steer his thoughts away from the shelter. Hoping to soothe her he maintained an almost continuous monologue, telling her of his youth in Nebraska, of his hurts as a boy, of his flying and even of Sally. He told her that he knew too well what it was like to be in pain and how the worst of all pains was loneliness.

Caressing her cheeks the slow, rhythmic movements of his hand and his weariness led him into a near trance until, without realizing what he was saying, he told her how he yearned for love of any kind. "We do not last very long on this earth, and I don't know whether that is good or bad. But I can tell you that a person who is not loved is near dead."

When at last her breathing became regular he bent down and closed her moist eyelids with his lips.

THIS night Moravia went home early because his sense of frustration had become overwhelming and he believed an obsessed man was not always a clear thinker. He needed a shave and a bath and his spare pair of glasses. And the comfort of his Marsha, although he wondered how he was going to tell her that her husband, who she had often claimed was the most unflappable of men, had so lost control of himself that he had whipped off his glasses and slammed them down on the desk. The total result of his pique was a broken lens—plus some release of dangerous steam.

His surrender to passion occurred as a culmination of minor defeats beginning with that pussy-cat Stiller, who he thought should be selling neck-ties, and the later discovery that Stiller was the last pilot who might have stood a reasonable chance of locating Number Fourteen and his passenger.

Then, as if Stiller's arrival had triggered some malicious intent in nature, the whole area weather had gone to hell.

Reports had come in from as far away as Salt Lake City; from everywhere within conceivable range of Fourteen's airplane. Who knows, Moravia had speculated, maybe Fourteen had found himself on top of an overcast and decided to turn directly east . . . or west? Or had, for some inexplicable reason, decided to head south?

"I want them all," Moravia demanded, "reports from anywhere within a four-hundred-mile circle. The whole picture."

Now he thought bitterly that he could as well have

asked for a single report since they were all nearly identical. Snow . . . low ceilings . . . poor visibility. No transient aircraft had landed and usually no aircraft of any description had landed. Everything west of the Rockies was locked up tight. Everywhere the noises created by those few outside endeavors still attempted were muffled by the continually falling snow. Moravia hated the new silence surrounding him. It savored too much of death.

The minor calamity of his glasses somehow made Moravia feel better in spite of the fact that he was obliged to hold everything he wanted to read at arm's length. By late afternoon he had managed to assemble what should have been an efficient search force. Two Ryan M-1 aircraft had been offered by Pacific Air Transport and every pilot they had volunteered for the search. Also standing by were two private airplanes based in Boise, a taper-wing Waco and a Curtiss Oriele plus their pilots. There were three of his own Stearmans now waiting in the hangar beyond his office and the men to fly them were eager to go.

The Air National Guard DH-4s from Spokane had been forced to turn back because of the weather. Moravia now considered them as an ultimate reserve.

Yet it had all been useless. Not a propeller was turning and as night came it was obvious that nothing whatever could be done presently. If the forecasts were correct only a limited effort could be mounted on the morrow.

When the full realization of his helplessness finally struck him, Moravia had slammed his glasses down on his desk and, as he thought immediately afterward, made a horse's ass of himself.

Now within the warmth of his home Moravia took off his artificial leg and allowed it to thump against the bathroom floor with what he liked to think sounded a satisfying note of defiance. Then he lowered himself gently into the tub Marsha had prepared for him. And he thought that of all the aviators he had known both in the war and afterward, Fourteen was the most appealing. Was it because they were both handicapped— a sharing of perpetual misery? Moravia thought not. There were no unspoken secrets between them and physical impediments were too personal to be easily shared. They were something to live with and you simply learned to tolerate or face disaster.

Floating comfortably in the tub Moravia regarded his stump and thought that it was much easier for people to accept a one-legged man than a two-sided face. Only the very brave would dare imagine such a tragic event that it would leave them with a face like Fourteen's. A face was entirely and specifically personal, the owner's mirror of himself displayed before the outside world.

The mask Fourteen was obliged to wear reflected nothing except a ruin. And yet, Moravia thought, although ruins were always sad they usually held an aura of mystery. You wanted to know more about a ruin than was normally exposed.

While he paddled his foot back and forth making wavelets on the warm water Moravia regretted that he really knew so little about Fourteen. He decided that if he survived he would try to know him better.

Whereas a man like Stiller would forever be just a blood and bones piece of machinery in the whole enterprise, Moravia doubted if he would continue to identify Fourteen as simply a number. In the future, if there was any future for the man, he would make a conscious effort to think of him as Jerry. He would invite him to the house for one of Marsha's special dinners, but he would not sentimentalize over his most recent misfortune because that was not the way of aviators. He would say, "Jerry, I never gave you a moment's thought. In fact while you were freezing your ass off, I was basking in a nice hot tub."

*   *   *

DURING the night the pilot slept fitfully. Once he heard someone screaming and he thought it was the girl, but when he rolled over and started toward her he realized she was asleep. Then he knew he had been dreaming and afterward he was almost afraid to try once more for sleep. I just cannot stand one more scream, he thought, whether it be real or imagined. I have got to tell the girl never to scream again while we are together because it gets to me so. I have got to explain to her somehow that any kind of screaming just does me in because it was the last sounds my student made just after we crashed. She can make other noises if she has to, but if she starts that screaming I am just not sure I can hold on to myself.

He turned his head and felt something hard beneath the mail sack and he knew it was the gun. He resolved to try hunting again. Maybe, just maybe, there was something out there that would make a meal. The damn gun had been a nuisance ever since Moravia hired him. And now there was nothing to aim at.

Lying in the darkness he mentally counted the pills in the little bottle. If he remembered correctly there were six left. That might be barely enough for another day and a night. Then what? She would scream again?

He wished he knew more about anatomy.

There must be a nerve pressing on another nerve or maybe a whole bunch of nerves twisted in her back. That's the kind of ignorance you get for falling in love with flying and not going beyond your first year in college. Dummy.

Maybe if he pulled on her legs or the upper part of her body, if she would stand it—maybe he could relieve the pressure and ease the pain. The trouble was that the least little back movement seemed to be more than she could tolerate for even a few seconds.

He forced himself to count his resources. Despite his trouble starting fires, the box of matches was still half full. There were three chunks of chocolate left.

Small. There was an unlimited amount of pine needles for tea, but their bitter, rancid taste made it questionable if they might not better enjoy pure snow water. If there were any berries or nuts or any other food in the vicinity which might sustain human life then he had not seen it. Incredible, he thought, that two nice people could starve to death on an American mountain in this day and age. But it sure as hell was happening.

What seemed to be the only solution was as obvious as it was frightening to think about. During one of his attempts to get away from Heather's murmurings and whimperings he had made an excursion across the plateau and continued until he came to the steep side of the mountain. He had floundered down through the snow for ten minutes to test his endurance and found himself in poor condition. As he waited to catch his wind and for his heart to stop pounding he almost convinced himself that it would be absolutely impossible to descend the mountain while carrying a girl who could not tolerate movement.

By the time he had made his way back to the shelter he was exhausted. He told himself, Look, walking in deep snow is tough labor even if you're going downhill. You have got to organize your thinking and be realistic. But right now controlling your thoughts is like balancing mercury in a flat dish. While you should be concentrating on a brilliant solution to this problem you are busy composing a letter to all mail pilots recommending they carry an axe. And what are they supposed to do with the axe if they crash? Chop down a tree and build a new airplane?

And while you're at it, he thought, you might apologize to the girl. What kind of a man are you to cut her short when she asked what would happen if no one came today? And if no one comes tomorrow? And capping it all by saying that by now for sure her mother would be very worried.

He had said, "She asked for it. Anyone who would

send their precious little daughter away in an airplane ought to expect at least some worrying. There was a perfectly good train you could have taken. Now shut up—"

What kind of a man said things like that to a little girl who hurt?

Now, when sleep would not come he thought, You don't, for God's sake, make remarks like that to people in trouble—even adults. If anything, her mother should be censured for sending her daughter away in an airplane piloted by a fat-head who seems incapable of doing things right.

WHEN the first hint of light filtered through the parachute silk the pilot crawled outside the shelter and saw that it might be a fine day. Venus was still visible, as were a few stars to the west, and there was not a cloud in the sky. There was no wind where he stood, but a plume of snow trailed south from the top of the mountain. A north wind usually brought clear weather.

He thought, this will be the day if they are ever going to come, but he decided against sharing his hopes with the girl. If they did *not* come, then there would be no recovery from her disappointment.

He had removed the magnetic compass from the Stearman on the previous afternoon. Now he poured a little of its alcohol content on his kindling and soon had a snapping fire. The ease of starting it greatly cheered him. He was beginning to make do . . . successfully. ·

In spite of the fine fire it took him almost an hour to make enough snow water for tea and he was reminded of the altitude while he waited interminably for the water to boil. If anyone came for them today or any other time, he thought, they were in for a long climb. The altimeter on the Stearman read four thousand five hundred feet, but he mistrusted it. The glass face was smashed and the impact of the landing could have made it inaccurate.

He sprinkled the pine needles in the water and smashed them against the bottom of the landing light receptacles with a stick. He crawled inside the shelter and presented the girl with the hot receptacle along with a chunk of chocolate. He took a second piece of chocolate for himself, the first food he had eaten since he left Elko.

He wondered if he could explain to Heather that unless he had something to eat he was sure his remaining strength would not last through the day. He decided against it. I must be her knight on a white charger, he thought, even though my horse is dead.

"Mind if I join you for breakfast?" he asked smiling.

He saw her try to return his smile and his hopes were renewed. She had not uttered a sound since the screaming last night. Maybe everything was going to be all right.

He held her head up so she could sip at the tea more easily and her helplessness nearly unnerved him. "What's the matter? Cat got your tongue again? The least you could do is make some comment on my cooking. Just remember all chefs are sensitive and our feelings are easily hurt."

She swallowed a gulp of tea and took a bite from the chocolate he held in his hand. At last she said, "Don't you think it would be better if you left me here and went to get help?"

"I couldn't do that. Absolutely could not even consider it." At least he was as quick in that response as he had been with some of his previous snide remarks. It was the screaming. He could stand anything but the screaming.

"Why not? Probably I would be all right."

"It's the probably part I don't like. It's a long way

to the nearest town. It might take me two days just to get there."

"Could you take me with you?"

"I thought about that, but I don't see how it would work if you can't move a muscle."

She was silent for a long time and as she sipped her tea he watched her eyes which were aimed directly at him and unflinching. And he thought her eyes were looking very old. Like a thousand years old, he thought.

He took a bite of the chocolate and masticated it very slowly, relishing the taste, swallowing as slowly as he could manage.

In spite of the sensual pleasure he enjoyed in the single piece of chocolate he soon became uncomfortable. For he realized she was watching his every move. Finally he asked, "Why are you looking at me like that? If you have something to say, say it."

There he was being snappish again. Fat-head. Why not just tell her it seemed like it might be a nice day outside?

"I am looking at your face. You are a very handsome man."

He knew now that instinct and long practice had caused him to keep the bad side of his face turned away from her. When he had picked her up at the airport his helmet had covered some of his affliction and since then when her pain and the dim light in the shelter allowed her to see anything at all, she could only have seen flashes of his misfortune.

He deliberately turned his full face toward her. He was feeling fine now. The chocolate had given him a huge jolt of strength. For an instant he thought he could conquer the world. "Look at me now," he said so easily he could not believe his daring. "Still think so?"

He watched her eyes, seeking the revulsion he was certain would be there, but he found only the same determined and peculiarly ancient stare.

87

"Yes, I think so, Jerry. You are beautiful because you are. I know all the things you have done for me. Now I want to ask you to do something else. I have been thinking about it ever since last night."

"Okay. Whatever it is I'll do it."

"Don't leave me here to die by myself."

He caught at his breath. He must be hallucinating.

"Whoever . . . what in the Sam Hill are you talking about, girl? Why, whoever even suggested such a thing? The way I have it figured you aren't going to die for a long time . . . eighty, maybe ninety or more years. You'll be an old lady with a hundred great-grandchildren. Besides, they're bound to come for us today or, if not today, maybe tomorrow or the next day. All we have to do is sit right here and wait."

"And slowly starve, Jerry? You haven't had anything at all to eat since we came here."

"I just had a big chunk of chocolate. I feel like a tiger."

"You had two bites. That isn't enough for a grown-up."

"What makes you so sure? What are you, a nutritionist or something? Why, in the big war some prisoners didn't get anything to eat for a week. As long as we can make water from snow we'll be all right."

"Did you fly in the big war?"

"No. That is I didn't get overseas where the shooting was. I trained down in Texas and by the time I was through so was the war."

"Then you have never killed any person?"

"No." If I was being completely honest, he thought, I might qualify that. There was always and would forever be that student he had failed to save from himself. "Now what is it you want me to do for you? Ready for the bathroom?"

"If they don't come for us today I want you to go down the mountain . . . by yourself."

"I thought you said never to leave you."

"I won't be here." She paused but her eyes remained fixed on his. "You have that gun," she said softly.

He reached out and took her face in his hands and he looked at her for a long time without saying anything. Finally he pinched her cheeks very gently and said, "Listen to me, my little friend. I don't know what kind of fairy tales you were brought up on, but you have no right to even think for one split second in that way. If your back wasn't hurt, believe me, right now I would turn you over and spank your little bottom so you would never forget it. Now you wipe away any more of that kind of thinking. Get it right out of your mind and I never want to hear another word on the subject. We are in this together. Is that perfectly clear?"

Jesus H. Christ, what kind of a world was this when an eleven-going-on-twelve little girl asked a guy to put her out of her misery with a gun? Or anything else?

He saw that she was weeping and he took the sleeve of the teddy bear and dabbed at her tears. "And don't bawl, for the love of Mike. If there's one thing I can't stand—"

He looked about the shelter, nearly frantic for something to divert her thoughts. This was horrible, a little girl thinking like that. At nine damn o'clock in the morning! He had to stop it.

"Heather, listen!" He scrambled across the shelter and brought back the mail bag he had been using as a pillow. "Let's read some more mail. If we have the same luck we had yesterday we'll hear about other people's troubles and ours won't look like anything. We'll think we're on vacation."

He took out a handful of letters and held them out to her as he had done before. She hesitated, yet he saw that she was making a deliberate effort to recapture her spirit.

She selected one of the letters and he opened it for her without taking his eyes from hers. Difference . . .

distraction . . . anything to get things rolling again. She absolutely must be forced to think of the real world and realize it was still there. So, he thought, must I. There is no inevitable.

Heather said, "This one is not very interesting. It's about money again and it says, 'Dear Sir: I understand you want to buy my Hereford bull Domino, but you only want to pay three hundred dollars for such a fine animal. Domino is out of Magic Lamplighter and his sire was the grandson of the famous Augustus . . .

" 'Well, Mister, you got to realize you can't buy an animal like Domino for peanuts. He is a very enthusiastic breeder and will chase your heifers all over your place until they are plumb tired. Now when it comes to sex, Mister, Domino's semen . . .' "

"Let's try another letter," he said hastily. "I'll choose this time since you don't seem to have much luck."

He thought, This shelter is only a long nightmare. The real world is in these sacks, and, by God, I am going to keep her there reading letters all day if I have to. If she returns to the real world maybe her back will improve and maybe her mind won't go off the trolley. Maybe we can wait this thing out in style.

He chose an envelope from the mouth of the sack, slit it open and handed her the letter. He was pleased to see that it was several pages long.

She studied it a moment. "Gee, this is nice handwriting. Nice and clear and it isn't even Palmer method. I'm going to tell Miss Atcheson about this one—"

"Who is Miss Atcheson?" He did not really care, but if Heather was already thinking of something she might do in the future, then that was progress.

"Miss Atcheson is my English teacher. She says we have to make big loopish stuff like in the Palmer method, but I would like to write straight up and down sort of like this."

She flipped the first page at him so he could see it. Then she held it to her nose and sniffed. "It smells good. That's what I'm going to have someday, Jerry. Some really smelly stationery."

Good, good, the pilot thought. She is planning. Now she has something to hold on to.

He wished he had some cause to feel the same.

"Okay," Heather said with new brightness. "Here we go. It starts out, 'My Dear Mrs. Tracy: This is the most difficult letter I have ever written in my twenty-five years of life, yet I feel it imperative to share our mutual sorrow.

" 'I suppose there was nothing really so different about your Jim and my Jim except his capacity for love. I suppose, but I shall never be sure. Certainly he was a most extraordinary man.

" 'Forgive me now that Jim is gone if I feel the need to write to you. Please be tolerant of this stranger you may despise because I was for such a short time another Mrs. Tracy.

" 'It seems to me no one can teach anyone how to love. We learn of love's existence very early, but where and how do we learn to give it? I must confess confusion now that I have been able to take my love for Jim out, hold it tenderly in my hand, and look at it. How dare I, now that he is gone? Well, I just do.

" 'I don't know why Jim was killed and I survived— I've tried to think why and only become further confused. In time I guess the physical Jim will fade from my memory and perhaps I will even meet another man with whom I'll want to share this precious life. Yet even if that should happen Jim will always be with me in the gift of love he left, and I will be eternally grateful for his legacy.' "

Heather paused and said she felt sorry for this lady. She also said there were a lot of big words coming that she was not sure how to pronounce.

"I'll just say them any old way so we can get the idea."

"Sure. Go ahead full steam," the pilot said.

"All right, now . . . she says, 'Is it not so that every person creates their own version of love? Some allow it to wilt and others nurture it to full strength and keep adding on to it. And usually they build a fortress that cannot be destroyed.

" 'Now I realize how love is available to anyone who will open their arms to receive it. Jim taught me that and he was dealing with a shy and rather wary apprentice.' "

Heather took a deep breath and whispered that on this page there were some words she had never seen before in her whole life or even in English class, for heaven's sake.

He urged her to read on and be damned to the torpedoes.

"Okay then, here goes . . . 'Now, after the two years I had with Jim, I think the love between a man and a woman is like one of those old-fashioned ka-lei-do-scopes? . . . the kind of cardboard tube you turned or shook and then looked in one end and found you would create all kinds of different patterns. Some caused you to actually cry out in such wonder and delight you never stopped to think they were all created out of the same crystals. Our love was like that . . . as I suppose yours was . . . sometimes all joyful, you might say all red and yellow dancing across each other and other times soft and serene with the colors mauve and deep blue-green. It just depended on how we turned the crystals that day, or hour, or minute . . .

" 'Just before that awful night, Jim asked me if I would mind living in Ireland if his job took him there again and I said, well, I don't care where we live . . . on the moon or Manitoba. As long as we were a unit my happiness would remain unbounded. At that time I could not imagine living without Jim and certainly never thought I might have to try. Then so suddenly there was no choice.

" 'Don't worry, Mrs. Tracy. I'm not going to show up at your front door some day just so we could have a good cry together. From what Jim told me I gather you must be a very private person and it is very difficult for relative strangers to share grief. Also, at this time you must hardly be in need of my tears which are stubborn about drying. No amount of self-spanking for self-pity seems to keep the salt off my cheeks. But I will stop . . . I *will*. I think people who know how to love are able to conquer anything they desire.

" 'Also, Mrs. Tracy, I hardly think you need a sermon on love as so recently discovered by a twenty-five-year-old late bloomer. So this little epistle is really intended as just a reaching out of my hand . . . to touch the woman I never knew, but shared Jim. Sincerely, Janet.' "

MORAVIA was elated.

This morning, the kind of morning to reinforce a man's faith in some kind of supreme manager, proved the weather people were worse than economists at protecting themselves against any eventuality. They were on-the-other-hand people. This would be providing this was, that is on-the-other-hand such and such did not occur. Marvelous, he thought now, as he surveyed the pale blue winter sky through his office window.

Like a little boy selecting sweets from a bounteous display Moravia moved from side to side along the large window, squinting first toward the north and then the south, making sure his eyes told him the truth, daring the sky to present him with the sight of a single cloud.

Now, by God, and no thanks to the weather people who had been predicting low ceiling and poor visibilities for all of this day and probably tomorrow, there could be proper search for Number Fourteen. All along the line to Elko the weather was reported clear and Moravia knew from his rising barometer that it was almost certain to remain so for at least a few days.

"All right, my friends, let us proceed," he muttered softly. He was watching the flashing propeller blades of two Stearmans warming up on the ramp in front of the maintenance hangar. The pilots, Wheeler and Iversen, were already in their cockpits bundled to the eyes against the cold. They were good men and not encumbered with aeronautical doubts like Stiller. If they saw anything worthwhile below, Moravia knew nothing short of the earth opening and swallowing the objects would prevent them from further investigation. They would proceed to the same general area where Stiller had thought he might have seen "something" (such as it was, he had at least provided a clue), and they would coordinate their flying to avoid working over the same territory.

Two additional Stearmans would be searching out of Elko to the south, east and west just to cover the chance that Fourteen might, for reasons still unknown, have chosen to fly in any of those directions.

The two remaining Stearmans would handle the regular mail.

Now that the weather was clear four National Guard De Havillands were due in Pasco by noon *if*, Moravia thought, they could get their Liberty engines started in the cold. They were water-cooled engines and Moravia liked to think their pilots had protected the radiators against the cold temperatures. Even so the Libertys would be a beast to start, with at least three men locking hands in a "daisy chain" as they pulled together on the enormous wooden propeller blades. Moravia planned to dispatch the De Havillands locally, then they would search southward from Pasco. A ranger who lived near the base of the Blue Mountains east of Pendleton had called to say he had seen something flashing on one of the summits. A rock reflecting the wear of a glacier fifty thousand years ago? A bird with a white wing? A ranger with a bit of mica in his eye?

Who knew? Even the most improbable must be investigated. Moravia did know that Fourteen could be down only a few miles from where he now waited so impatiently.

They must all hurry, he thought. The days were all too short in these latitudes and clear weather brought its own curse. Tonight would bring the stars, and just as surely for the homeless, agonizing cold.

THE pilot was silent for a long time after Heather had finished reading the letter. It was as if he was waiting for her answers to the multitude of questions now confusing his thoughts. He glanced at his watch. How did it get to be almost ten o'clock? Another day already well worn and still he had not accomplished anything.

Now where were all his brave projects? Where were the necessities to keep them alive and most of all, where were his guts to keep this awkward situation from calamity?

He watched a full minute pass, and as he watched another he could only think that two minutes of his blundering life had expired. I am older by two minutes, he thought, but not any wiser.

Heather also remained silent, fingering the pages of the letter.

"What did you think of the letter?" he asked finally. He wanted to hear her say it was the most intriguing letter she had ever read because most certainly it had been written by a woman he longed to know better.

"I think she must be the opposite of you," Heather said. "She doesn't squirm around when she says something about stuff like love. She just opens herself and lets it go . . . and I like that."

"What was her name again?"

"Janet. What I want to know is, who is the other Mrs. Tracy?"

"I gather she must be the mother-in-law."

Heather studied the letter a moment, then she said, "No . . . maybe not, because she says here it is very difficult for relative strangers to share grief."

"She could still be Jim's mother. The name is the same. She called her Mrs. Tracy, didn't she?"

"Okay, but then she says right in the beginning that they have never met. And here near the end she says, 'I gather you must be a very private person' . . . so she must not know her very well. Doesn't a wife have to meet her husband's mother?"

"Not necessarily."

"Well, that's a funny way to be married. When I get my husband I want to know what his mother is like. Maybe she would be a witch and that is something I would like to know."

"And I say your wisdom is beyond your years. When are you going to tell me the story of your life?"

"All eleven years and eight months of it? You want me to tell you how I got an A on my geography exam and I didn't even know where Bolivia was?"

A blob of sunlight flowed through the parachute silk and the pilot took it as a signal of overall improvement. The weather was clearing and more importantly the girl was beginning to think in the world of futures. If she could somehow be locked onto this letter or anything else tangible, then that niggling little notion that she was playacting and telling him only what she thought he wanted to hear would go away.

"Do you suppose," Heather asked, "that Janet could have written this to *another* Mrs. Tracy . . . like maybe the man had two wives?"

"I doubt it." She was studying the letter so intently he thought that if he could get the powerful subject of food off his mind he might even be able to smile.

He said, "Didn't she say they were going to live in Ireland or somewhere? She wouldn't write that to another wife and besides, the husband doesn't sound like a bigamist."

"What's a bigamist?"

"You might say it is a man or woman who can't count."

"Listen to this, Jerry. Let me read the last line to you again . . . She says she is just reaching out her hand . . . 'to touch the woman I never knew, but shared Jim . . .' "

She stared at him over the top of the letter and asked him what he thought of that.

He said, "Maybe she was a former wife, in which case they must both be very special women."

"You mean the husband must have got a divorce from the first Mrs. Tracy?"

"Could be." He was becoming bored with Heather's curiosity and her preoccupation with only one of the letter's revelations. He tried to remember what the woman had written about love.

"I've got it, I've *got* it!" Heather's voice rose triumphantly. "Right here it says . . . 'please be patient and tolerant with this stranger who was for such a short time *another* Mrs. Tracy.' She has to be his second wife writing to his first!"

Heather held out the envelope. "The person's name is Mrs. James Tracy and she lives in Portland."

Heather slipped the letter back in the envelope and said, "You're not paying attention. It's no fun if you don't care what the letter says—"

It was true that he had not been listening to Heather's discoveries. Instead his ears were tuned to a sound he thought at first might be a trick of the wind. It was almost inaudible against the soft whirring of the pine boughs, but it was there, increasingly distinct with each passing moment.

He sat with his head cocked, his whole body tense, his eyes roving from side to side as if he were examining every seam in the parachute overhead.

"What are you looking at?" Heather asked.

"I'm not looking at anything. Do you hear what I hear?"

"I don't hear anything."

She pretended to listen as he pushed himself to his knees. Then he began a very slow crawl toward the entrance. He paused often, listening, his head tilted toward the silk above him.

Heather called out to him. "Where are you going? Aren't we going to read more—"

"Shut up!" he said harshly. "Don't make a sound."

"But I don't—"

"Shut up, Heather, or I'll stuff a fist in your mouth—"

As he continued toward the entrance he heard a stifled whimper behind him. He ignored it, he had to . . . because another sound had absorbed his entire being. "I think," he whispered, "it's very far away, but I *think* I hear an airplane . . ."

MORAVIA was talking on the telephone with Elko and he was reasonably satisfied with what he heard. "We had trouble starting one of the Stearmans. A magneto. So we kept it here and dragged out one of the old Swallows. Number Five. And we needed the Stearman for the mail. By the time we got everything squared away it was eight o'clock."

"Are they all in the air now?"

"Yes. But Montgomery, who's flying the Swallow, has never flown one before. It was in the back of the hangar when he came to work about a year ago and it hasn't flown since."

"Is he nervous about it?" Moravia was mindful of

the Curtiss K-6 engine that had powered the Swallows. Their record for reliability was dismal.

"Hell, no. He says he'll fly a manure shovel if he can just find Jerry."

"All right. How long have the Stearmans and the Swallow been off the ground?"

"About an hour. They should return for fuel about noon. I'll call if they've seen anything."

"Call me anyway. Get them back in the air as soon as their tanks are full."

"They'll need some rest. They'll be cold."

"Not as cold as Jerry."

Moravia was pleased that he had hesitated only briefly in referring to the pilot as Jerry rather than Fourteen. Indeed, he was progressing. He was making progress toward a new portrait in his mind. He saw now the erasure of a mere number and in the man he had just called "Jerry" he viewed the strangely refreshing arrival of a human who also knew what it was to suffer total personal defeat. The portrait, already gathering color and mood, became fascinating. Now Moravia found the beholding of it so enormously satisfying that he castigated himself for being so long in creating it.

He said into the phone, ". . . keep searching until dark."

By the time he had emerged from the shelter the pilot knew that he was not just imagining a sound he longed to hear. When he had gained his feet he stood listening. His every instinct concentrated on a sound that he thought would probably be inaudible if he had not been half-listening for it in the first place. For two nights and almost two days now he had literally dreamed about this moment.

The sound faded and again there was silence except in the pine trees. He thought the wind must be fighting the sound waves and destroying normal echoes. Sweet music swept away from an audience of one.

He ran a few steps through the snow. What for? Was the music any clearer here . . . ten paces from the shelter?

He paused and listened again, holding his breath lest the slightest sound compete with the one he so yearned to hear.

But now there was no man-made sound.

He waited, craving for the rhythmic beat of an aircraft engine. He could hear it in his mind, the pulsations, the lazy reverberations as the propeller slapped at the air, yet he knew he was not really hearing anything except the soft squeaking of his leather jacket as he turned his head slowly back and forth.

Yet inside the shelter he could have sworn he heard an airplane. Now the girl would be upset because he would have to go back inside and tell her it was just a fire drill. And she would probably whimper worse than ever and he would begin to think seriously about jumping off the mountain now . . . before rather than after he went crazy.

The fire drill was ready to go but it had to be a one-time event. It would take him more than half a day to gather enough good wood for a second fire. There must be no false alarms.

He had stacked his best wood in a pyramid below the shelter. The oil to pour on it was in the crude container he had made out of a piece of exhaust stack. It was in the ready position near the pyramid and should make fine black smoke that a blind man could see for miles. That is if the oil was not too congealed to burn, and if the gasoline he had salvaged and preserved in a similar container would make the green wood burst into flame.

There were a lot of ifs.

Yes! There . . . over there! It was. It absolutely was. And the sound was approaching. No question.

He reached in his pocket for the box of matches then remembered he had left them in the shelter. In his glove. To keep them dry. *Now* was when they should have been handy.

IT was when she was alone like this that the idea kept returning. Miss Phipps, who taught World History, would understand. Once she told the class about Joan of Arc and how she chose to be burned at the stake rather than keep on fighting whoever it was she was fighting.

Heather tried to remember who Joan was fighting, but failed. Yet she could see right now and very clearly just exactly what happened that afternoon when Miss Phipps told about Joan of Arc and class was dismissed. All the girls took turns backing up to the stairway post and being Joan of Arc, with their hands clasped in front of them and having that holy look in their eyes while they died for the thing they believed in.

Now this pain was like it must be for people who were burned at the stake. Heather of Arc. No one in the whole entire world could ever, *ever* say she was a crybaby.

Every time Jerry went outside and stayed away to do whatever he was doing the idea came back. And it was getting stronger every time.

Heather turned her head and stared at the place beside her where Jerry had been sleeping. The fabric from the airplane was still rumpled where his body had pressed against it. The mail sack he used as a pillow was at the far corner, and protruding just a little from beneath it was a piece of leather.

No one in the whole world, no matter how much they wanted to be brave, could stand this pain. Like Joan of Arc, some people were better off dead.

She reached out and found the edge of the fabric

with her fingers. By flexing her fingers she pulled the fabric toward her. It slid so easily over the packed snow no one in the whole world would ever believe it.

The mail sack with the leather underneath it moved with the fabric. When it came within reach she pushed the mail sack aside and her fingers closed on the leather holster. She brought it up slowly and held it directly in front of her. Then she took the gun out of the holster and shivered because it was so cold to her touch.

She thought about Jerry. No one in the whole entire world would ever believe what an extra extra special man he was. Like the Prince of Wales or one of the great men Miss Phipps talked about. He should go down the mountain while he still had time. Of all the people in the whole world that anyone could possibly think of, he should know that someone loved him. Like one of those kaleidoscopes? It just depended on how the crystals fell into place. People who knew how to love could accomplish anything, just like Mrs. Janet Tracy said in her letter.

She experimented by poking the muzzle of the gun at her heart. Then she tried it against her forehead and flinched at its coldness. A different kind of pain.

Now the engine sound was unmistakable and it was approaching rapidly. In his haste the pilot fell down twice as he struggled up the rise toward the shelter. He thought he had a minute, maybe two minutes to fetch the matches. Then it might be too late. His anxious mind suddenly seized upon the fact that he was hearing an in-line engine. It certainly sounded like a Curtiss K-6, which meant that it would be on a Swallow. What difference did it make when seconds were wasting? Get the damn matches and forget everything else!

At the entrance he fell to his knees and scrambled

quickly into the shelter. Once inside he raised his head and looked into the muzzle of his gun.

"Go away," Heather said quietly. "Go back outside, Jerry."

He hesitated, unbelieving. His body remained motionless.

"What do you think you're doing?"

"Go away, I said. I mean it, Jerry."

He watched her eyes and saw that she was totally serious.

"Heather. That thing is dangerous. Put it down."

He started to reach for the gun, then changed his mind. He saw that her finger was on the trigger. "Heather. Listen. There's an airplane coming. I've got to build a fire right this minute. It may be our only chance."

He tried to keep his voice even, but he heard the fear in it.

"I love you, Jerry. I want you to live. Please go away—"

He knew then what he had to do and indecision left him. He forced a smile. "Okay. If that's the way you want it."

He moved as if to back out of the shelter, then halted. "Can I get the matches?"

She nodded slightly. Hoping to protect them against dampness he had kept the matches inside one of his flying gloves. Now he reached for the glove and took out the box of matches. He turned momentarily until he was facing away from Heather. Then still holding the glove he spun around, whipped the glove hard and knocked the gun from her hand. It slithered across the fabric and he grabbed it instantly.

He tucked the gun in his waist and started for the entrance. Panting from his exertions he glanced back once. He was going to say, "You are naughty, girl."

Then he saw she was weeping.

He scurried out of the shelter and ran down the slope

to the pyramid. He forced himself to think only of a fire, but his thoughts tore at his concentration. Was there anything else in the shelter she could use to harm herself?

Now the engine sound increased rapidly in volume.

As he took a match from the box he stole a glance at the sky. Bare . . . blue. He saw there was still time for a fine fire. Burn down the damned mountain.

He struck the match. It fizzed, but failed to ignite. He took out another, repeated his action and was appalled to see the same result. What kind of matches did they make these days?

He took out a third match and saw that his hand was trembling. Calm down and stop panting. There is still time.

He forced himself to breathe deliberately and slowly as he struck the third match and cupped his hands around the feeble flame. All right, all right, this was it. Here now was man's first and best friend . . . ready to comfort him, ready to start a huge fire that would signal a true friend aloft. He would have to be stone blind not to see the black smoke that was about to be.

Now the sound of the engine echoed against the side of the mountain and seemed to fill the entire area with its resonance. Beneath the engine reverberations he could hear the faint sibilant note of the airplane's slipstream. Yet he dared not look up from his task.

He cupped his hands and held the match protectively until a few wood chips took fire. He reached for the oil container, determined not to pour it on too soon. That would be the dunce act of all time, he told himself—build a fine fire and then douse it at just the wrong time.

He stole a glance at the sky. By God there he was. Coming right on target. He could not miss. Hallelujah. And it *was* a Swallow. Unmistakable.

He poured the oil on the fire and threw the container aside. He rose to his feet and jumped up and down in the snow, waving his arms and shouting as if the pilot could hear him.

The airplane passed across the sun and he was blinded momentarily. Then he was able to see it again, so close he could see the oil stains along the belly of the fuselage. He yelled with all the power in his lungs, clasping his hands together and raising them over his head in a victory salute. He yelled until he became giddy from lack of breath and finally he waited impatiently for the first hint of the airplane's banking.

The Swallow continued in a straight line, directly toward the summit of the mountain.

He glanced at the fire. There was a good column of brown smoke rising from the pyramid even though there was still little flame.

He looked up, his hands still poised above his head.

"He will turn now," he thought. "He is just checking for possible down-drafts before he commits himself."

He saw in his mind how the Swallow would bank and then descend in a graceful dive and whoever was flying it would give him an unforgettable "buzz" job. Then he would fly back to Elko and give his position on the side of the mountain and probably by this afternoon a rescue party would be on the way. It was going to be that simple and at the worst they would arrive some time tomorrow.

He found that he was holding his breath. The Swallow dipped a wing, first to the left and he thought it was the start of a bank. But then the right wing went down and came back up. He thought it must be rough up there. Okay, my friend. Take it easy. I've got plenty of time. Who was it? Iversen? . . . Pomeroy? Maybe Montgomery, the new guy who was said to have a law degree.

Hey, wait a minute!

The pilot's hands broke their union and began a frantic waving. For the Swallow continued on a straight-line course to the north.

"Come *on* . . ."

The pilot's mouth fell open and a strange cry escaped him as he watched the airplane continue toward the summit, glisten for an instant in the sun, and then disappear.

Suddenly there was no sound of an engine. Suddenly there was only the immaculate sky, the sun, and the mountain.

He stared at the peak for a long time, half hoping the Swallow might reappear, although he knew that it would not. How could anyone miss? How could anyone even with bad eyesight fail to see a man standing in the snow on the bare side of a mountain? And now a great brown pillar of smoke? How could he miss seeing that?

He dropped his hands and bowed his head.

"I must be very small down here," he thought. "Very, very small . . . an invisible runt."

He stared at the fire and the smoke and knew that he had been too late in starting it. By two or three precious minutes.

He looked at the summit again and all around him and down into the valley far below. And he began to laugh, softly at first and then ever more forcefully.

His eyes filled with tears as he shook his fist at the mountain and then at the blue sky and the sun. And he yelled with all the power left to him. "Right . . . right! I *know*. I am a nothing, a for damn sure *nothing*."

He continued to laugh as he shuffled up through the snow toward the shelter. And he became aware that his merriment sounded almost exactly like Heather's whimpering.

HE lay on his back using the same mail sack for a pillow. His eyes were wide open and he was staring at the fading pattern of light on the parachute silk above him. He told himself that now the time had come, yet he was unready for it. How much longer could he procrastinate?

He forced himself to visualize the present activities of the Swallow's pilot. Whoever it had been made no difference now. It was more important to realize he would probably be having coffee in Elko or Boise or even Pasco if he continued that far and he would be explaining to Moravia, or someone who would relay the fact, that he had not seen anything of special interest.

Was the plane he had seen actually out looking for him and his passenger? Or was that just a wishful assumption?

BECAUSE of the sun's position he had been unable to see the side of the Swallow's fuselage which might better have confirmed his belief. U.S AIR MAIL would have been painted along the side just as it was on the Stearmans. And since there was only one line flying the mail in this area it was logical to assume your own people were looking for you. They must be using everything available including some of the elderly Swallows that had been retired. All of which should fall into a logical pattern—except that it did not. Who could foresee that a two- or three-minute delay in starting a fire might be so crucial? Who would ever imagine that a simple little girl would spend even one minute thinking about killing herself?

And how could any pilot miss seeing so much smoke against snow? Easy. They were not equipped with eyes in the back of their heads. And who could say now that the Swallow flown by a man with faulty vision really did belong to the line? It might have been a private aircraft. It could be someone flying for the

Forest Service . . . or whatever. And that pilot would not necessarily know anyone was down. He could be just having a fine flight on a clear day and if his lips were not frozen he might even be whistling away to express his pleasure and why should he bother to look down?

If it had been someone sent out by Moravia the pilot might say, "I've been over such and such an area and I did not see a thing that looked like man or beast. Nothing, and it was a perfectly clear day so I could see for a couple of miles on each side."

Would Moravia then ask if he could see directly underneath him? Because of the location of the lower wing on the Swallow and the forward angle of view from the cockpit, visibility straight down was poor. Moravia had never flown Swallows—they came along after his flying days were over. Would he have asked if the pilot zig-zagged so he would not miss anything, or just assume he would not fly in a straight line? Would a new man, say, like Montgomery who had never flown a Swallow, be so preoccupied he would not realize how much he was missing below until it was too late?

Next stickler and a really sharp one. After the pilot of the Swallow found nothing and made his report it would be logical for Moravia to abandon this area and move on to another. He would be pressed for time, men, and airplanes, and he would say, "All right, let's get on with it because we have a whole hell of a lot of real estate to cover."

There would be no logic in resurveying an unproductive area.

The pilot whispered to himself, "Blaming a little girl is not going to get you out of this fix."

He was reminded that he was not by himself, for Heather called out to him. "What did you say, Jerry?"

"I didn't say anything."

"Jerry, I want that horse over there."

"You want what?" She was mumbling and still whimpering and he thought he had certainly misunderstood her.

"I want that horse. The black one. I've always wanted a black horse . . ."

He rose to his knees and shuffled to her side. He looked into her eyes and saw they were vacant of expression. She seemed to be looking right through him.

"Now what's all this about a horse?" he asked. "There's no horse—"

Heather pointed and screamed. "The one coming at us! It is going to run over us. Stop the horse, Jerry. Stop him before . . ."

She screamed again and he covered her mouth with his hand. She struck out at him and bit his hand. He jerked his hand away.

"The horse, the big black horse," she repeated over and over again as he sucked at his bloody finger.

"You sure have sharp teeth," he said. He was so shocked at her behavior he barely felt the pain in his hand.

How do you bring delirious people back to real life? Quick now, doctor.

Her voice rose in another scream. Instinctively, he bowed his head and clapped his hands over his ears. I will not listen, he thought.

"Will you please stop screaming," he asked as evenly as he could manage. If it was necessary to humor delirious people, then he would do his best to go along with the presence of a horse or anything else she fancied.

Heather shook her head violently and choked on the sputum in her throat. He reached out to raise her head and she pushed him away.

She started to claw at her face and she mumbled over and over again, "My horse . . . keep him away . . . keep my horse from hurting me."

As he pulled her hands away from her face she tried to strike out at him, but she could only slap at his leather jacket.

They struggled in silence and he was astonished at her strength. Finally their heavy breathing eased and when at last she subsided he pulled off his belt and tied her arms to her sides. When she realized her confinement she began to sob violently and for a long time she seemed not to hear his attempts to soothe her.

Later there was a time when she lay cradled in his arms and he thought his reassurances sounded more like the mumblings of a madman.

"Quiet down or the neighbors will complain. You can't go on making a fuss like this all night. It isn't civilized. Sure we are in trouble, but haven't you ever heard about people who are shipwrecked and just sang until they were rescued? Sing, don't yell. Let's make that our motto."

He debated giving her another pain pill. Maybe they triggered her delirium. He felt her moist brow and decided that if she had a fever it had now left her.

He rocked her gently in his arms and he kissed her hair frequently. He could hardly believe the sound of his own voice as he told her that he loved her and as he continued to caress her hair he could not understand how he could say such a thing so many times, to an eleven-year-old girl. "I need you, Heather. I need you more than you could ever imagine. I have forgotten what holding someone in my arms is like."

She quieted in the very last of the day's light and when she looked up at him he knew she was herself again. She seemed surprised that his face was so close to her own.

He reached down and removed his belt from her arms, kissing her eyelids closed so she would not see what he was doing. When he had finished he saw her smile.

"Show me your dimples, but don't look so wise," he said.

Heather said, "I'm sorry to be such a trouble-maker." She brightened slightly. "I've been thinking about Mrs. Tracy . . ."

For a moment he could not relate the name to anything and wondered if she was starting to slip away again.

"I think the second Mrs. Tracy wrote that letter about love and all that stuff to the first Mrs. Tracy because they both loved the same man. She was trying to share her trouble with the first Mrs. Tracy because she must need a friend."

"What are you, a psychiatrist or a fortune-teller?"

"Mrs. Gooch says I'm forthright. My mother told her I have powers of deduction because it runs in the family."

"Who is Mrs. Gooch?"

"My math teacher. May I please see the letter again?"

He knew exactly where the letter was because he had placed it carefully in the pocket of his jacket.

His intention had been to read it again. He thought it odd that now it had become *the* letter while all the others were of little interest.

He held the letter out to her and after studying it a moment she said, "This is the part I like best where she is telling about how she is going to stop crying. Right here she says people who know how to love are able to conquer anything they desire."

"Maybe she's right."

"Okay then. How about if I pretend to be in love with you, then maybe I can stop being such a nuisance?"

"You're not a nuisance. What would I do without you?"

"If Mrs. Tracy can stop bawling so can I. And if

I can stop maybe we can go down the mountain to-gether."

"There are a lot of reasons why it's too risky."

She handed him the letter. "Read it again, Jerry. I bet when she was in school Mrs. Tracy got *forthright* on her report card."

LATER he estimated his physical strength and found it wanting. By his reckoning he might have one more day at the most before he would be too weak to do any-thing but wait. And to wait, he thought, was to die.

Even now he rose only slowly from his fabric bed and signals of his general lethargy were everywhere about him. When the pyramid fire had burned itself out he had not rebuilt it. Available wood seemed much too far away. Nor had he refilled his containers with oil and gasoline. He had contrived a crude siphon using a length of rubber tubing from behind the Stearman's instrument panel, but the last time he had sucked on it there was so little remaining in the fuel tank he brought up more air than gasoline. The fumes made him want to vomit. The fire in the shelter had gone out twice and each time he had been a long time reviving it.

Soon, he thought, he would start finding excuses not to leave the shelter.

As the light faded he thought, Even now I am hesitating.

He crawled outside, taking the letter with him. The sun had gone and the snow squeaked beneath his boots as he moved away from the shelter. He noticed a new chill in the air, or was it hunger that so lowered his resistance?

Now he longed to be alone for a time, alone with the letter which had somehow become the voice of a third party on the mountain. Camp Tracy, he thought. Will the second Mrs. Tracy please join us for dinner? We can offer you superb pine-needle tea and I will split half my piece of chocolate with you.

He halted in the twilight and stood looking down at the distant valley below. There was no wind and from the look of the sky he supposed there would be little chance of wind in the morning. Still, he must remember the snow would have a hard crust and if he broke through with his burden then that might be the final calamity. Twenty miles at, say, a half-mile per hour just to be realistic . . . say forty hours. That was almost two full days of plowing through heavy snow if they were lucky.

It was impossible. The girl would not be able to hang on to his back for half that long.

He took the letter from his jacket pocket and began reading. Now he was sure he could visualize Janet Tracy. She would be small and spunky and dark-haired. Her words gave away her enthusiasm for all things. She would know humility because she obviously had the courage to censure herself for self-pity.

"These are the things," he said softly to the evening, "that I understand."

He decided that Mrs. Tracy must also know what it was like to barely escape being killed and he thought that people who knew what that was like were never the same afterward.

Now, after what he thought must be his tenth rereading, he found he particularly liked what she said about holding her love for her husband in her hand.

He folded the letter carefully, reinserted it in the envelope, and placed it in his jacket pocket. As he buttoned down the flap of the pocket he knew very suddenly what he must do. There was a way to take Heather down the mountain . . . maybe. Why, during all his vacillating, had he failed to think of it? All of the risk was still there, but at least they could die trying.

He made his way back to the fuselage as quickly as he could. He wanted the last of the light to see all of the things he had to conquer in the morning.

FAR to the west of the mountain, beyond the Quinn River and Desert Valley, a spur of warm, humid air had separated from a major low-pressure ridge flowing eastward over the Sierras. The spur developed into a small front in itself and brought rain to regions which had only recently been buried in heavy snows.

The antelope found the rain beneficial since it quickly reduced the snow pack and made movement much easier for such grazing as there was. Likewise did the deer and the elk benefit and to some extent the badgers, porcupines, beaver and other small creatures who inhabited the wilderness.

The warm air seeped in during the night enveloping the higher altitudes first and then flowing down into the valleys. For most of the night there was little effect except the reduction of the snow below belly level, but by dawn those animals who were hungry and alert to every feeding opportunity became unusually wary. For now they heard a sound familiar to them, the hiss of small snow slides slithering down from the higher peaks and the occasional roar of big avalanches thundering down the mountains.

The animals moved gingerly, heedful to the slightest uncommon alarm, for generations of experience warned them of the new hazard. Their long-developed instincts urged them to avoid the southern sides of the mountain.

LONG before the first light came through the parachute silk the pilot awakened. He listened for any sound from beneath the bundle of cloth that was his teddy bear. And he was grateful that the girl was apparently still asleep. There were three pills remaining, just enough he hoped to last her down the mountain.

He rose to his knees as quietly as he could lest he wake her. He shivered uncontrollably for a moment. Had they really been on the mountain only two nights and two days? It seemed like months since he had last flown.

He crawled to the fire and took off the gloves he had worn through the night hoping to at least keep his hands warm. The embers were cold and he debated starting another fire. It took such a long time and every minute of this day would be needed.

He glanced at his watch and decided he had no choice but to start another fire. They would need water and they might as well start with hot tea. Six o'clock. For two days and nights the hours had dragged. Now there would be no more waiting and he thought, if what I am about to do is a mistake then it will be my final mistake. But I am strong this morning, stronger than I have ever been since the landing. I have the hunger of an animal, but I am still strong.

He started a little fire with the handful of chips he had saved from the previous afternoon. It smoked badly and he thought he might hear the girl complain, but there was no sound from the teddy bear.

He crawled back to her, listened to her breathing for a moment, then kissed her gently on the cheek. He wanted to say, "I love you, Heather," but he could not bring himself to say it even in his mind. "People would not understand," he whispered, "and even you might not understand if you could hear me."

A moment later when he turned away and crawled toward the entrance he thought the cure for his long loneliness might be attainable. On this morning, he thought, I can attain anything.

Once outside he was disappointed in what there

was of a dawn. There was hardly more light to the east than west and all of the sky was covered with dark cloud. Yet it was warm, so very warm the snowflakes which struck his face melted instantly. He was grateful. Now he could work without gloves and his task could go much faster.

He rid himself of the little liquid that was in him, then returned to the fire with a landing-light receptacle full of snow. He piled several pieces of broken ribs from the Stearman's wing on the fire to make a fine blaze—and there was no longer any need to keep them as an emergency supply. Then he awakened the girl.

He asked her if she was going to lie in bed all day and he called her "lazybones" and they held hands until she was fully awake.

"Do you hurt?"

"Yes."

"Do you hurt too much to sit up?"

"Yes."

"But you have to be in a sitting position when I take you down the mountain."

She hesitated and after a moment pressed his hand with her fingers. "Then I will sit up."

"Are you ready for a test flight?"

She smiled and nodded her head, but he saw the fear in her eyes and he thought, If she screams just once then we are just not going to be able to do it. "Do you want to try a pain pill first?"

Again she shook her head, this time in refusal. He saw her lips were compressed in anticipation, her little jaw was thrust forward, and her hands were doubled into fists.

"All right, we'll take it very easy," he said as he slipped his hand beneath her shoulders. "Now, if you can't stand it we'll have to think of something else."

What else? he wondered. There was barely time and energy for what he had so carefully planned.

He watched her face as he lifted her shoulders very

slowly. As the teddy bear fell away from her he was reminded how small she really was.

"All right, so far?" he asked.

She nodded affirmatively, but her lips were quivering and he knew she must be hurting.

"Not much further to go," he said, and he marveled that at a moment like this he would instinctively keep the good side of his face toward her.

He paused. "You're almost there," he said. "Do you want to go for all the way?"

"Yes. I'm okay," she said, and her voice was so faint he could barely hear her.

He eased her forward a fraction of an inch, then another until she was sitting erect. "Can you stand it? This is the approximate position you'll be in all day long. If you can't hack it we have to know now."

She swallowed and he looked away from the distress in her eyes.

He eased her forward very slightly and waited. "Well?"

"I can do it. I *will*."

"Congratulations." He eased her back to a prone position and tucked the teddy bear around her. "We'll have a big breakfast, then I have about an hour's work to do. Then, my friend, we'll go down the mountain."

He saw that her eyes were filled with tears and he very much wanted to wipe them away. But he also thought, I must not weaken now or through all the hours to come. We can't win bawling together.

When the water was hot he broke a handful of pine needles into small pieces and pressed them against the side of the landing-light receptacle with the screwdriver. He crawled back to Heather, propped her head on a mail sack, and asked her to hold the receptacle while he served the main course. He broke the last piece of chocolate in half and advised her to chew slowly since the portions were so small. They sipped alternately at the receptacle, passing it back and forth

117

between them with solemn formality. They said nothing to each other except with their eyes and that, he thought, was quite enough. For he knew that people who were about to put their lives on the line were rarely given to conversation.

When they had finished he took the receptacle and told her to be patient. Then he started his usual crawl for the entrance. He had just turned away from her when he halted. He listened to a rumbling sound outside the shelter. It grew in volume, passed in the distance, and then ceased abruptly.

"What was that?" Heather asked.

"I don't know."

"It sounded like a train going by. Every day at three o'clock the Union Pacific goes through Elko and it sounds just like that."

"I hardly think that's what we heard."

He continued his crawl toward the entrance. He had never before heard such a sound and he did not like it.

His spirits rose as he emerged into the full light of the morning. How warm it was and altogether it did not appear to be a bad day for their expedition. The peak of the mountain was obscured in cloud yet the visibility in the lower slopes was good. He could see a hump of bare granite far below which previously had been covered with snow and the dark configurations of the many streams were now clearly defined.

The pilot crossed his fingers as he approached the Stearman's aft cockpit. Now, he thought, I will need a sack full of pure luck to accomplish phase one.

He brushed the drifted snow away from the seat and the fastenings which secured it to the fuselage. And he thought, God almighty, why did they have to build this airplane and everything in it so strong? Then, as he fingered the double retaining nuts for size and the six bolts that held the back of the seat to the airframe, he chided himself for being unreasonable as well as ungrateful. No, he decided, I would not vote for a less sturdy aircraft even if I never suspected I would have to put one down on the side of a mountain.

Thanks to Moravia's foresight he was not bare-handed. Yet the over-strength of the seat fastenings was going to make removing the seat difficult when the only tools available were a screwdriver, pliers, and one crescent wrench.

In his mind he had given himself one hour to accomplish the task. It was almost two hours later and his knuckles were bloodied before he removed the final nut, knocked away the last bolt and heaved the seat out of the cockpit. He put it down in the snow and sat down in it. He licked at the blood on his hands and remembered that the actual weight of the seat was a factor he had neglected to include in his plans. Good God, it was heavy.

His scheme, so nicely envisioned during the endless nights, had been to fix the parachute straps to the seat, then slip his arms into them in the normal way. The rear side of the seat would rest against his back with the seat facing away from him. Heather might be at least tolerably comfortable and her weight would be evenly distributed. When he felt the need to ease the weight on his back he would find a slope or something of equal height to the seat and back up to it. The seat could be adjusted. If he needed a longer rest, or Heather wanted to lie down, the harness could be slipped off his shoulders and the seat removed.

Still, the weight of the seat even without Heather in it was shocking.

He sat in the snow thinking of some way he could carry the girl without the seat, but everything he imagined was even less practical. Finally he rose and shrugged his shoulders. He said aloud, "Hello, Jerry. Here's your chance." Then he formed his fingers as if he were holding a glass, and whispered, "Here's to love."

He decided to dispense with the seat belt, which would save weight. Heather would have to hang on if the going got rough. Securing the parachute straps to the seat went more easily than he had expected, yet it was mid-morning before he carried his creation to the entrance of the shelter. Just outside he had prepared a waist-high mound of snow. He placed the seat on top of it and made sure it was firmly set. Finally he adjusted the parachute's straps so he could slip his arms through them without moving the seat itself.

Weary from his continuous exertions he promised himself he would sit down and rest for five full minutes before he brought Heather out of the shelter. He had caught himself staggering occasionally and he had experienced moments of vertigo which infuriated him; who needed to ride on a merry-go-round? If he could only lie down and close his eyes for a short time, then maybe the damn turntable would stop.

Suddenly he changed his mind about even a short delay. For at the opposite end of the plateau where a gigantic jaw of granite projected from the mountain, he saw an ugly mass of snow and rock tumbling out of the skirt of the upper cloud. It moved swiftly downward, topped like an ocean comber with a crown of froth and it vomited into the valley below. Moments later he heard the roar of its passing.

He went at once for Heather.

SOMETIMES Moravia thought his little operation might be a sort of leftover casualty station from the Great War to save the world for democracy. He was at his window again, brooding on the disappointments of the search for aircraft Number Fourteen and the luckless man who had been its pilot.

Had been? Perhaps if he had been killed instantly—the kind of death every aviator preferred if it must come—then he was not so unlucky after all. Ever since Moravia's own first time aloft the phrase had always been, "If it's going to happen I don't want any fire and I don't want things coming to pieces bit by bit with a long ride down while I watch it happen. Just let me go straight into a mountain or something, then one minute I will be and the next minute I will not be." It was not a prayer, Moravia mused, but it echoed the philosophy of every pilot he had ever known from his days in France to the present ominous-looking morning.

There was Number Fourteen's face, of course, which had hardly been decorative to the establishment. Now beyond the window was the mechanic Rohrbach, missing one hand thanks to the propeller of a "Jennie." Long ago some fool student who sat in the cockpit became confused, although he claimed to have misunderstood Rohrbach's command to make sure the magneto switch was "off." Instead the student left it "on" while Rohrbach backed the propeller and the damned OX-5 engine fired. With the usual lack of logic, Moravia thought wryly.

The propeller removed Rohrbach's left hand and he was very lucky his head did not follow the same route.

Working on the tail section of a Stearman just inside the hangar door was Pickering, who had a permanent stoop. Moravia considered him the best aircraft rigger in the business, a man who tuned flying wires and the consequent set of bi-plane wings as truly as a master harpist caressed his instrument, but Pickering had not always been noted for his tactile skill. Only a few years ago he was "Wild Charlie Pickering," star of state and county fairs.

After thrilling the crowds with his antics as a clown wing-walker who came within inches of falling from his perch, Pickering finally overdid his pretended clumsiness. While he was clambering around the landing gear of a Hisso Standard the airplane hit turbulence, Pickering miscalculated, and "Wild Charlie" fell to certain death. God fell with him. For the projectile that was Pickering landed head first where the straw from the livestock exhibits was deposited. When he was pulled out Pickering was a mess of manure, but he was alive and the fact that he had smashed four lower vertebrae after a fall from more than two hundred feet was considered by Pickering himself as only incidental.

Finally there was Carson, known as "Kit," who had just come into view. He was wearing his teddy bear and would be flying the regular morning mail, hopefully through to Elko. Carson was an old-timer. He had flown with Pershing in Mexico when the Army was not at all certain what to do with airplanes, much less how to classify aviators. When he had finished his chore south of the border he went north to Canada, joined the Royal Canadian Air Force and flew against the Germans with the likes of Billy Bishop, and Quigly and McCall. He had been shot down, crashed between the lines, and spent the night in a shell crater. At best it was the wrong place and wrong time. Sometime during the night he got a whiff of mustard gas and, with no mask to protect him and a long wait before he was hospitalized, he eventually lost one lung.

At least, Moravia thought, Carson's missing anatomy did not show and visitors to the line, including those Post Office inspectors who stuck their noses into everything, would not be further convinced that the business of flying was no business at all.

Moravia returned to his desk and started thoughtfully at the map which covered it. There were now large areas which he had cross-hatched lightly in pencil. These were the squares his pilots had over-flown and presumably seen everything below. And reported nothing of interest. There were still some considerable areas where Number Fourteen might have gone down, the Strawberry Range to the west of Baker, for example, although it seemed incredible that he would have strayed so far off course. There were also the Wallowa mountains northeast of Baker, Indian country and again most unlikely.

Presently the National Guard De Havillands were searching through the valley around Pendleton and would work south during the day. Two of the locally based Stearmans were already over the Blue Mountains and should be returning soon for refueling and further assignment. Unless, of course, they spotted Fourteen.

Moravia tried not to let hunches influence his study of the possibilities, and he was contemplating the area where the Powder River joined the Snake when he heard a discreet knock on his door.

He turned to see Stiller standing in the doorway, his teddy bear draped over his arm and his helmet and goggles in hand.

"Good morning," Stiller said in his guarded way, and Moravia thought that of all his charges this man, who bore not a scratch from his profession, was probably the most severely wounded.

"I didn't know you were scheduled to fly this morning," Moravia said.

"I'm not, but I will if you want." Stiller moved into the room warily as, Moravia remembered, he did everything.

"I've been thinking," Stiller said, "and I talked it over with the wife and she suggested I come and see you about it again if I really feel that way . . ."

What way? Moravia mused. Now, in the midst of what appears may be a tragedy, my life is going to be illuminated by whatever the hell it is Stiller's wife thinks ought to be done. Remarkable that she has loosened her silken chains long enough for her precious mate to come to the airport on his day off. Is that why he always refers to her as *the* wife instead of using the possessive?

"What's on your mind?" Moravia asked.

"Well . . . I've been up most of the night worrying. I told the wife what kind of flight I had yesterday . . ."

she always wants to know all the details, and I told her I *thought* I really might have seen a piece of an airplane down through that hole north of Capitol Peak. Well, the more I thought about it and the more I discussed it with the wife the more certain I became that I did see something. Then, when we were lying in bed last night and the lights were out, I found that I could sort of visualize things better and now I am just about ninety percent sure I did see something down through that hole . . ."

For a long moment Moravia managed to remain silent. Then he said, "Well, I'll be goddamned."

Moravia resisted the temptation to describe in a series of colorful phrases exactly what he thought of Stiller's character. Instead he bent over the map and beckoned Stiller to join him. "Show me again where you think you were."

Stiller made a circle on the map with his finger. "I was somewhere in here. I am sure of that."

"Okay. I'll train the morning's mail. You take the last airplane we have and get yourself back there. By afternoon you should have a lot of company because as they become available I'm going to send every airplane we've got to join you."

And just in case you become wishy-washy about having a good look this time, Moravia thought, I will put a bird dog right on your tail. For that job I will send Carson, who has already used up most of his lives and does not baby those he has left.

NEAR the end of the plateau the pilot halted momentarily and looked back at the shelter he had created. From even this little distance it was not nearly as imposing a structure as he had assumed. Now it appeared to be no more than a small scratching on the snow-covered mountainside. He could see the folds of the parachute draped over the fuselage and a piece of the Stearman's tail sticking up, but the wings were so far removed from the fuselage and were so concealed by the trees he had to reassure himself they were not just two additional irregularities in the snow. If you knew objects were there, he thought, you might see them, but otherwise—?

"Say goodbye to your happy home," he said over his shoulder.

Heather said, "Aloha."

"Where in the world did you get that?"

"My uncle lives in Hawaii and when he came to see us last summer he was always saying it. That's goodbye in Hawaii."

"Do you ever forget anything you're told?"

"No. Especially not if I like it."

"How are you doing back there otherwise?"

"I'm still here. Am I too heavy?"

"I'm glad you've been on a diet."

They were able to talk lightly throughout the first hour and then the silences between them became increasingly longer. In time he knew the effects of the pain pill he had given the girl just before he hefted her to his back were wearing off. It had always been the same, first the silence, then the little whimperings, and finally the agonized screams. There was one pill left.

While the sun was still at the zenith their descent remained surprisingly easy. The pilot found a gully leading off the plateau and the footing was good until it steepened and joined with a stream bed. Here there were countless huge rocks and house-size boulders interlaced with withered brush and broken trees all swept together, and he realized nervously that the debris must have been left by a recent avalanche.

He looked up at the hulking mountain. From where he had paused it appeared more sinister than ever and he saw that the jumble of rock and forest he must now negotiate was strewn across the bottom of a natural chute.

He had not rested since they left the plateau, but this was no place to linger. Across the chute he saw what appeared from a distance to be easier going. Less than two hundred yards away there was a long slope, clear of trees and angling gently downward. Now the afternoon sun polished the virgin snow of the slope and it appeared to be no more than a few minutes trudging around the hodge-podge of obstacles. Once there he would rest.

Two hours passed and he was still in the chute. It seemed that every time he found a way across, some insurmountable object stood in his way and he was forced to retreat. He had lost count of how many times he had arrived back at the same place. The stream flowing down the middle of the chute was the principal villain. He was afraid to cross where it was deep and where it was shallow the stream ran so fast he thought it might knock him off his feet. With the weight of Heather and the chair it was doubtful if he could rise again.

He checked his watch. Two o'clock. They were already three hours behind his hoped-for schedule and he estimated they had made less than two miles of progress. He listened to the rumble of another avalanche; so many had shaken the silence of the mountain that he had almost ceased to notice them. He knew his strength was ebbing much faster than he had supposed it would, but he was committed now and he was convinced that unless he continued, this ugly ravine could become their tomb. Now they would most certainly have to spend the night high on the mountain instead of in the valley as he planned.

He considered returning to the shelter and making a fresh start in the morning, but he doubted if his strength would hold through the uphill climb.

"Heather," he said quietly as he continued to explore

a new way out of the ravine, "we are not doing very well."

"Are you very tired?" she asked.

"No. I'm fine." He tried to picture himself perched in a seat on the back of a man with legs of lead like his own and decided nothing would be gained by telling her the truth.

"I've been thinking about the letter," she said. "I especially like that part where she says every person creates their own version of love. When I think about that I sort of forget my back because . . . well, if a person thinks fancy and just uses a little imagination, which Miss Livingstone says I have plenty of, well, that might just as well be describing you and me."

"I take it Miss Livingstone is one of your teachers? Sooner or later I guess I'll get to know them all."

"No. She's our next-door neighbor and I don't think she knows much about love because she's an old maid."

"Aren't you being sort of rough on Miss Livingstone?"

"Yes. I know I shouldn't be because she's very nice, even if love has not been her specialty—"

He joggled the seat badly as he worked his way along a ledge of rock that was bare of snow and promised to provide a new exit from the chute. He heard her cry out and then she stifled the sound.

Hoping to distract her, he asked, "Does Miss Livingstone discuss her personal life with you?"

There was no reply from behind him. He waited, then tried again. "How would you know what Miss Livingstone's specialty might be?"

Again there was only silence and he thought, I must ignore whatever is happening back there and keep going. The only thing that counts is to get out of this place before dark.

Later he heard her voice. "Jerry . . . ?"

"I'm listening." Not really, he thought, but failing

fast. I'm like an airplane wing at the point of a stall and for damn sure I'll soon spin in.

"Jerry, are there people who specialize in love?"

"You sure are a question box. I don't know how to answer that." And, he thought, I don't have the strength left even if I did know.

"I don't want to be like Miss Livingstone."

"No chance. You won't be."

"According to that letter from the second Mrs. Tracy I guess there are different kinds of love and you can sort of take your pick."

"I'll have to think about that for a while." He would not, he knew. He must not permit himself to think about anything whatsoever except getting down this damn mountain. It must be down—down all the time and every step in the right direction counted. Ratio of steps to altitude lost? Say average of twenty-degree slope so multiply by four . . . equals sixteen thousand steps. That is, if you can keep going in a straight line, which is impossible. Okay, divide by say thirty steps per minute . . . equals eighteen hundred steps per hour. At least nine hours hiking with no rests. And that would be just to the bottom of the mountain. Not really anywhere. Jesus H. Christ!

As he worked his way cautiously from boulder to boulder and around the ravaged trees, he sensed that he was no longer entirely himself. While he seemed to have command of his body, his mind wandered out of control; he was no longer able to consider the distance they had to go as real. Nine hours? What with switch-backs and other delays and some rest here and there it was going to take more like eighteen hours, to where? To a nice little village, of course. That was just waiting to make them warm and comfortable. Right down there in the middle of nowhere. A village that maybe did not exist.

He moved automatically. The dull aches caused by the parachute straps bearing into his shoulders became almost intolerable. I cannot go on like this forever, he thought, but I'm doing it anyway.

At last he found a way across the stream and Heather made her first sound in a long time. She asked if she could have a drink of water, so he backed up to the end of a fallen tree until it took the weight of the seat. He eased off the shoulder straps and moved around the tree until he could see Heather's face. And for a moment her blue-green eyes held him spellbound. She said, "You're so tired. I am so sorry for you—"

He reached down impulsively and took her hands in his. And he could not help himself, although he knew he must be hallucinating, when he brought them to his lips. "You are a beautiful woman," he heard himself saying, "and I love you very much."

He knew his mind was shifting from the actual to the unreal and, he thought, I can just stand here and watch it perform as if I were a third person.

He saw her attempt a smile and instead of the confusion he had expected he was sure he heard her say, "I love you, Jerry, and I hope we will always be together."

He moved quickly to the stream, cupped his hands together and caught up some water. He brought it back to Heather's lips and tipped his hands slowly as she drank. He asked if she wanted more and she shook her head.

He went back to the stream and went to his hands and knees to ease his own thirst. And as he bent over the stream he saw his face reflected in the water.

He pulled back. He had forgotten his face. He *had* been hallucinating to such a wild degree that he had thought he was like other men . . . momentarily. The effect of altitude? Or lack of nourishment?

He closed his eyes, bent his head over the stream for a gulp of water and stood up. He returned to Heather and found she had been transformed. Now she was only an unhappy-looking little girl bundled in an over-large flying suit. Mucus was dripping from her nose. He took out his handkerchief and wiped it away.

Now for the first time during their descent he noticed that his hands were filthy. Was the good side of his face equally revolting?

"Are you ready for some more?" he asked flatly.

"More water?"

"No. More walking." He did not welcome the irritation in his voice, but it was there.

"Can I have a pill?"

"No. You're turning into a junkie."

He moved around her and squatted until he could slip into the shoulder straps. He rose slowly until he felt her weight, then stood up.

He heard her ask, "What's a junkie?"

Still irritated he answered gruffly, "None of your business."

He left the stream in a few strides, then started down the open slope as rapidly as he dared. Between the creaking of his leather jacket beneath the straps and his own labored breathing he thought he heard the girl weeping.

He did not pause, but continued downward, his shadow long on the snow.

Never again, he thought, never again will I allow myself such pipe dreams.

CARSON was the last pilot to leave Moravia's office. The others—Pickering, Stiller, and Horton—had reported in after they had landed, and by evening Boyd and Montgomery had telephoned from Elko with almost identical findings. They had all spied the wreckage, but it was Carson in his rasping voice who best described what he had seen.

He stood pulling at his cold purple nose before

Moravia's desk, still in his teddy bear and boots, the red marks left by the pressure of his goggles still around his temples and cheeks while he said, "I must have circled the wreckage twenty times and I buzzed what was left close enough to wake the dead—pardon me, wake anybody in the world. I really knocked the place up at about fifty feet, no more, and I'm damned sure if anybody was half listening they woulda heard me. I saw the wings. They were smashed up between two trees . . . all to hell. Then there was the fuselage with his chute hung over it and it was all smashed and on its side—"

"Was the engine still attached to the fuselage?"

"Yeah. Sort of, that is. Of course everything is covered with snow and there isn't much left, but it would be a miracle if anybody got out of that one."

"But weren't there tracks in the snow?"

"The light was very flat when I finally got there so it was hard to tell. But I did see a place where it looked like he might have built a fire. But one thing is for sure. There is no sign of life anywhere around there now."

"Were there any tracks leading away from the wreckage? It seems to me that if he was strong enough to rig his chute over the fuselage he must have been mobile."

"Maybe. But the chute could have opened on impact and spread itself around. I damned near caught a wing-tip trying to get an angle where I could see into the cockpit and check if he was still in it, but with the fuselage on its side and the cockpit facing up the slope it was hopeless."

"But it did look like he built a fire?"

"It sure looked like it, but everything is so covered with snow that even when I slowed down to sixty miles an hour it was impossible to confirm anything except that it was Jerry's airplane. I could see the big Fourteen on the tail. No question about that."

Moravia lit a Caporal, sucked the smoke into his lungs and coughed gently. It would now be his unhappy duty to call the passenger's grandparents and her parents in Elko and inform them the airplane had been found. What else? That both occupants were undoubtedly dead? They would have died without pain, of course. Of all the times that Moravia had anything to do with notification of next-of-kin he could not remember a single instance where a relative was told the truth about the manner in which their beloved had actually departed. In this case he supposed he would follow custom. The pilot and his passenger had died instantly and painlessly.

As for Jerry, the man without a home, there would not even be the need for that. Moravia thought that he had best stop by his barren flat and see if there were any clues to people who might be slightly interested that their friend or relative "Jerry," whose last name Moravia was ashamed to discover had been quite forgotten until now—it was Amity; what a name for a man so out of harmony with the rest of humanity. The man who was flying Number Fourteen, has, you may be relieved to know, perished without suffering.

Not good enough. ". . . without *excessive* suffering."

"There are times," Moravia said, snorting smoke at Carson through his nostrils, "when I truly hate this business."

"I understand," Carson said, and Moravia knew that he did and was grateful for it.

Carson had left then, saying he was going down to "Fred's Place," the local speakeasy, and take on some whiskey.

Moravia sat alone and in silence until it was dark in his office. Finally he sighed and switched on his desk light because he knew he would soon be required to answer certain questions and he wanted to be prepared. He made a series of phone calls, making doodles with his pencil after scribbling down each number. Finally he located a Maxwell Foster at his home in Reno, Nevada, and told him about finding the wreckage.

"Since you're chief of the forest district I would like to know how soon you can bring down the bodies . . . that's assuming there are any."

"Wait a minute. I'm not even sure that's in my territory—"

"And if it were not are you telling me that you would ignore the situation?"

"You don't have to be so testy. I wouldn't consider sending a party up in that country until late spring anyways."

"Why not?"

"It's too dangerous. Avalanches, for one thing. The Forest Service is not equipped to—"

"The Forest Service is financed by the taxpayers and that includes your salary, Mr. Foster. We cannot leave those people up in the mountains until it is convenient and comfortable to bring them down. They have relatives—" At least one of them has, Moravia thought sourly.

"I would have to get authorization from Washington—"

"How long does that take?"

"Two weeks . . . maybe a month. But I won't recommend it at this time of year and they won't go over my head."

Moravia wiggled the Caporal between his lips so violently he spilled ashes on his sweater-vest. Someday, he thought, the world will be populated entirely by bureaucrats because all the real people will do away with themselves in frustration.

"Very well, Mr. Foster," he said slowly. "We will send our own party to the wreckage. And be advised that any assistance you might be inclined to offer will be considered a hindrance."

He hung up the phone and decided he felt much better. Now, he thought, it will do no harm to procrastinate. Bad news is easier to receive in the morning than at night. Furthermore, the bearer should be entirely composed himself lest his private sorrow multiply the grief of those entitled to it. They have lost a daughter, he thought, and I have lost a son and the combination is extremely volatile.

I will wait, Moravia thought, at least until morning.

He turned out the light, but did not move from his desk chair. He sat in the darkness for a long time, wiping at his eyes frequently and wondering why after so many years his missing leg still felt like it was there and why it even hurt when anger or sadness took him over.

Would it be so, then, that a body still hurt—after its rightful occupant departed?

ALTHOUGH the twilight lingered, the pilot knew, at last, that he was lost. He paused at the mouth of a narrow canyon because he realized that to continue on he must climb. How could this be? It was now obvious that for the past several minutes of recent memory he *had* been climbing . . .

From a distance it had appeared that the floor of the canyon sloped downward and offered easy access to the valleys below. That had obviously been an illusion he had held for too long. His whole mind must have taken a holiday for an hour, maybe more. Or sometime between his first acceptance of the canyon as a natural exit and this very moment when he stood so bewildered he must have fallen asleep. His feet and legs had kept going because behind him was the trail through the snow as proof, but the rest of him had apparently taken off for other worlds. You did not hike up to go down.

His eyes must have been open at least most of the time or he would have fallen down, but somehow the past few hours had been erased. Now he was suddenly aware that things were all wrong.

The canyon was blind. It terminated in a vertical rock face that rose at least a thousand feet. Not even a mountain goat, he thought, could find an exit from where he now hesitated.

"What's the matter, Jerry?"

"Shut up, Heather. Please."

He wanted silence, or did he really? Until just this damn second he had all the silence any man could ask for. Jesus H. Christ, was it ever quiet up here! What had happened to the sound of avalanches? Where were the birds and the beasts? How come nobody in any shape or form lived around here?

"Jerry? Is something wrong? You must be really pooped."

There she was again, needling when a man was trying to think straight. How would she like to know she weighed a ton and that a genius who could not think straight for more than ten seconds at a time just for damn sure could not believe what had happened in the last few hours? Or face up to it?

Now he recognized a sensation he had not known for a long time. All airmen experienced it at least a few times in their career and once their feet were planted firmly on the ground they were given to smiling sheepishly and admitting they had been "surrounded by lostness."

"We are in deep trouble," he thought he was saying in a whisper, but instead heard his voice booming across the snow.

"Why? What's wrong, Jerry?"

He was glad he could not see Heather's face. It was easier to think of her as just a weight on his back, something he could not get rid of no matter how powerful his desire.

"You tell me how things are in the caboose," he said, hoping to divert her long enough to figure out how the hell they had wound up surrounded by impossible obstacles. Not quite so. Just three of them were impossible. The fourth was beyond thought. If he turned right and avoided the canyon there was the edge of the slope and a straight drop down for God knew how many hundred feet. If he turned left he would hike smack right into the mountain itself. The canyon was obviously a dead end. Who said dead? Who thought that word?

"Things are fine back here, but it's getting dark."

"I can see that." I can see like a blind man and have just proven it, he thought.

She said something he could not hear clearly in spite of the hush and he wondered how he was going to tell her they had no alternative but to turn back and retrace their route, which meant a long up-slope climb. But to where, for God's sake? Where had the wrong switch been turned? Even if he would find it he could not possibly climb all the way back to the shelter and start over again.

Maybe I am going crazy, he thought. Where are all the locals . . . the bear and the antelope? I need directions to the nearest restaurant.

He turned around slowly and blinked at the trail his long descent had made in the snow. And he saw that he had not walked at all in an orderly fashion; the trail curved and recurved, snaking gracefully back up the mountain and finally disappearing over a rise. A drunk could walk a straighter line, he thought.

He was stunned at the prospect of reclimbing the mountain. It just could not for damn sure be done by *anyone,* with or without wobbly legs. Maybe the best thing to do would be to sit down and think things over.

He cancelled the notion. Somewhere in a book he had read something about men lying down in the snow and never getting up again.

"What was the title of that book?"

"What book, Jerry?"

He realized that he had spoken aloud again when a mere question had swooped through his mind. Oh, things were for damn sure getting hard to hang on to when your brain spilled everything right out on the snow. Hey there, mumbles, you with the cuckoo-clock mouth, when is the next announcement?

"Jerry? What's the matter? Why don't you rest for a while?"

"I'm afraid we would go to sleep and never wake up."

As the vapor from his heavy breathing formed momentary clouds in front of his face, he supposed he must have said the wrong thing and compounded Heather's worries. But dammit, he needed to share his troubles with someone close to him, and this was a world populated by only two people.

"I'm sorry," he grumbled.

"What for?"

"Never mind. I gave in to a need . . . just for the moment . . . forget it . . ."

"Do you still have the letter?" he heard her ask. "We could read it to each other and that would keep us awake . . . especially if we read the part about how every person had their own idea of love, sort of . . . I think I memorized that part."

"My friend," he said, keeping his voice as causal as he could manage, "I'm not only pooped, I'm lost. I guess the only thing we can do is to go right back to where we came from and find another way down."

She seemed not to have understood him. The tone of her voice sounded totally unconcerned when she asked, "When you were in school did you ever play that game where you cancelled out the letters in another person's name that were the same as in your own name . . . and that way you find out if the other person, which of course, if you happen to be a girl, would have to be a boy—well, you find out if that other person just happens to be the right person for you? Once

137

I tried it with Homer Grimstead who sits across the aisle from me and it came out all wrong. And sure enough Homer and I are always fighting about something. A while ago I did it in my mind with your name and it came out perfectly, so I guess that if I didn't make a mistake working without a pencil and paper . . . just cancelling letters in my mind, which is very hard to do . . . I guess somebody back here in the caboose loves you."

I must not give in this time, he thought. I must not slip away into another dreamland or I will never come back. "You understand what I said about going back up where we came from?"

"Yes. Maybe it will help if you think of the letter."

He reached instinctively for the pocket of his jacket, then dropped his hand. Somehow it was enough to know the letter was there.

He leaned toward the mountain and took a step forward, then another and another. At once he noticed the terrible demands in carrying his burden uphill. He bent far over to ease the strain on his shoulders and he sought every easement in the path he had made during the long afternoon.

Darkness came while he was still trudging upward, and he was grateful for what little illumination the stars offered.

Later he thought, I am just not going to make it for more than another few minutes unless I find a second strength somewhere. Or a third or a fourth?

His heart was pounding alarmingly, he gasped for every breath and clusters of tiny lights swam across his eyes. His legs seemed self-automated, moving up and down on their own, and occasionally he knew the same vertigo he had experienced during the late afternoon.

They came to a forest as he had anticipated, and still climbing he listened carefully for the gurgling of the stream where he had given Heather a drink. There was no sound other than his own labored breathing and, God almighty, there it was again, the stifled whimpering from behind. If she starts screaming, he thought, I'll just have to slap my ears until I'm deaf. I just can't stand one more yell. Just not a single one.

DEEPER in the forest there was almost no light and he nearly collided with trees only a few feet away. Their dark shapes reeled in front of his weary eyes and sometimes they joined together until they seemed to be pressing in and down on him. Hoping to shake off the sensation, he walked with his head held high, trying for glimpses of the stars, something, anything familiar and friendly.

He heard her say, "Jerry? I think you're going wrong."

"What gives you that idea? We're going back where we came from."

"We should be more over that way."

"What way? I told you we had to go back to the stream and start over."

"That's just it. The stream is over that way."

"You don't know what you're talking about. We should be there in a little while."

He paused. Holy simoleans, all I need right now, he thought, is advice from the peanut gallery. "Hey, you in the caboose. You can't tell a thing about where we're going from back there. Why don't you just go to sleep and not confuse things?"

"The snow is much deeper here and it hasn't snowed. And besides I saw the old trail turn off that way a while ago and I just thought, well, you knew a better way to get back where you wanted to go. That's all I thought. You don't have to get owly with me, Jerry."

"I'm not owly. I'm just tired. And I apologize." If

139

I were a real owl, he thought, I could see where I'm going.

He focused on the snow just ahead of him and was shocked to discover there were no tracks. He *had* wandered off somehow. He should have kept his mind on his business instead of becoming absorbed in the stars. "All right, my friend," he said slowly, "you win. Which way were you pointing?"

"If you turn around and go back down not very far . . . I know where there's a big hump of something under the snow and that's where you left the trail. The stream is off to your left . . . no, it will be off to your right when you turn around."

When he found his original tracks again he resolved to follow the stream no matter how his instincts argued. It was flowing dependably *down* the mountain and nothing else counted.

"I'm going to give you a medal in the morning," he said. "You are one smart little cookie."

"Remember my mother said I have a logical mind."

Slipping frequently and stumbling in the darkness, moving as in a long nightmare, he made his way slowly over and around boulders and through the chill tributaries which fed the main stream.

Following the sound of the stream as much as its darker hue against the snow, he slipped and fell frequently to his knees. Each time he heard Heather cry out in pain, and yet the immediate silence which followed helped him resist the temptation to lie down and stay. When he said he was sorry that he could not help his clumsiness, Heather said she could not keep from bawling sometimes because her back hurt her so, whether they were falling down or not. "But I promise, criss-cross my heart, that when we get out of this I will never, never bawl again."

At last they left the forest behind and continued downward along a more open slope. They came on a flat area where the snow was deeper and he decided it might be a road. Now, his mind drowsy with monotony, he heard Heather call to him as if from a great distance.

"Jerry! Jerry! I see something. Back there. Back where we just came from."

He paused. "What now?"

"It looks as big as an elephant. Or something."

He turned around and saw a dark shape against the snow. After only a few steps he saw that it was a truck, a lumber truck, he thought, and momentarily allowed his spirits to soar.

Heather said, "If it's here it's because someone lives near here."

"Not necessarily."

"Well, whoever owns it had to come from *some*place."

"That's logical."

"I told you I had a logical mind. And so if it's a truck we must be on a road. And the road must lead to *some*place."

"Okay, okay . . ." As he trudged toward the truck he found that he had a tendency to hold his breath. Just suppose he blew the horn and someone did appear out of nowhere to find out what was going on with their property? Just suppose they did live in a dry warm cabin and they would be led to it and this awful endless night would end.

His hopes sank as he approached the truck and he saw how the snow had drifted over the wheels. Near the door it was up to his thighs.

The door window was broken and he saw the cab was filled with snow. Yet still half-hoping, he reached through the window and pressed on the horn. The only sound was a whisper of wind through the cab.

As he leaned against the door—touching anything man-made seemed terribly important now—he heard Heather say, "Well, I don't care if it is old and fallen to pieces. If it got up here somehow . . . we can get down. That's logical."

He knew they had been in a valley for a long time, a month, a year; maybe forever. Here the terrain was smooth and almost level, and in the easier going his strength was somewhat renewed. Yet a layer of broken clouds now obscured the horizon and he had even more trouble keeping his equilibrium when he lost the stars. Now they were only occasionally visible through breaks in the overcast, and he thought that if he knew them better he would be more confident he was proceeding in the right direction. He tried to keep the Belt of Orion over his left shoulder, which should steer him in a westerly direction, but as the hours passed it climbed directly over his head and looked approximately the same from any angle.

He was grateful for the few planets which sailed through holes in the cloud cover and provided enough light to distinguish rocks and major depressions in the snow. Each time he became unbalanced he fell almost to his knees before he recovered, and each time he had less will to rise. It seemed as though he had never done anything else but plod through snow.

"How goes it back there?"

"I'm still here."

"I'm aware of that." How she managed to hang on through all his lurching was beyond his understanding.

"Are we lost again?"

"No. I don't think we have much further to go."

"Are you telling me a fib, Jerry?"

"Why don't you try going to sleep?"

"I hurt too much."

"Do you want a pain pill?" He wondered if he should remind her there was only one left.

"No. I don't want to be a junkie."

When Heather grows up, he thought, let us pray her husband never tells her anything he wants her to forget.

He found it helped to force his mind toward such

thoughts and the sillier the better. It helped to keep one foot slogging after the other when both had long ago lost all feeling. Now in his fatigue the length of his stride was becoming ever shorter and he was bent nearly double under his load. There were times when he was convinced he had actually fallen asleep and then awakened to find himself still slogging through the snow.

Hoping to keep alert, he tried various mental excursions, including several halting attempts to repeat the Lord's Prayer without error. He calculated the distance they had gone and the distance remaining to the town of McDermitt, but the numbers were based on his inexact knowledge of the crash site and the reckoning proved more discouraging than helpful.

During one period of fancy he matched Heather's age against his own and found she would be twenty when he reached forty-one and what was wrong with that? He was about to tell her he would wait for her, then decided against it. Heather would never reach twelve unless he concentrated on this one night alone. This was different than having an engine quit, an historic event over which he had no control. Now was now, his weary mind kept repeating. Now this very morning, or was it yesterday morning now, he had deliberately violated the prime rule of any crash and left the scene. Everything else had been a preliminary, he thought, and the main event for which you are entirely responsible is now.

When there seemed to be no conceivable end to his exertions he found distraction in trying to recall parts of the letter. He could remember certain lines verbatim and words that he would ordinarily shy away from and they seemed to prod his almost total exhaustion. Yet gradually he became aware that his thoughts about the letter were becoming more confused. The face he so often visualized in the snow was not the face of the letter writer he had pictured originally. Now she had become a woman he knew well. She appeared, vanished, and reappeared. She spoke to him in phrases apparently set to a metronome and her voice was sonorous and familiar. Later he discovered that the cadence of his stride had become a slave to her voice, and although he knew he had lost his self-control he found he was not interested in regaining it.

There came a time in the middle of the night when he could not force his legs to obey his commands for one more step. He stood wavering in the feeble starlight, regretting his weakness all the more because they had come to a barbed-wire fence and he knew it must lead to somewhere from nowhere. Now there was something to follow, but he could not follow anything. He knew he must relieve himself of his burden immediately or he would fall face down and that would be the end of things.

At last he slipped to his knees and leaned to one side until the weight of the seat was eased. He slipped off the shoulder straps and told Heather they would rest until morning.

"Why are you whispering, Jerry?"

"I don't know, I just can't talk—"

Still on his knees he made a shallow place in the snow and when it was done he pulled the seat away from Heather and eased her into the depression as gently as he could.

She reached out to touch his cheek and said, "I know how tired you are."

He realized suddenly that her hand had caressed the disfigured side of his face, the sunken area where the tortured skin stretched drum-tight over the twisted bones and looked so much like half a skull that he had never dared to suppose anyone would ever feel compelled to touch it.

He started to speak. "I . . ." but that was as far as he could manage. A new peace took him over, he was serene as he had never been before, but he could not find the words to tell Heather what magic she had performed. My legs are gone, he thought, and even the muscles that move my lips are limp and I don't care. At least this is the end of loneliness. This is the true life and everything else has been a nightmare . . .

After he had eased Heather down he waited for her to cry out but she made no sound. He adjusted the teddy bear protectively about her until only her nose and eyes were visible.

He kissed her on the nose and even in the vague starlight he could tell her eyes were smiling. Finally he lay down beside her and drew her to him for warmth and he thought, we love each other. We will not die here.

MORAVIA had fixed noon as the time he would abandon all hope for the occupants of Number Fourteen. The morning mail for Elko and the East Coast would be well on its way by then, the petty details of the line disposed of and the usual morning interruptions of his planned day would already have proved him a fool for ever attempting to discipline the immediate future.

Once noon had passed he would force himself through the gloomy business of telephoning relatives. He had already rehearsed his opening lines. "I am extremely sorry to inform you . . . If there is anything the line can do to make things easier . . . Of course our insurers . . ." Et cetera.

As for Jerry, the man without home or family, what to do? Make a telephone call to whom it may concern? Write a letter to General Delivery . . . Anywhere, U.S.A.?

The pilot's application lay on the desk before Moravia, and now he found it hard to forgive the number of blank spaces he observed, including "Next of Kin." At the time of hiring, of course, no one in the flying end of the company paid the slightest attention to application

forms. The experience of pilot applications were reviewed verbally, a far more reliable gauge than mere
hours recorded on paper. And who cared about a
pilot's schooling? If he could fly he could fly, and if
he could not he should not be allowed to kill himself
or anyone else.

Yet at times like this, Moravia mused, lack of paper
work was inconvenient. And goddamn the whole flying
business anyway. *Merde!* The war was long over. People should not die trying to earn a living.

Moravia glanced at the wall clock which he remembered some idiot before his own incumbency had bought
because it was the same style as was customary in railroad stations. Then he checked the clock against his
wristwatch and found they agreed it was thirty-three
minutes past eleven. Twenty-seven minutes to sorrow
time. *Merde!* It had been a long morning and it was
becoming interminable.

SOMEWHERE in the distance he heard Heather's voice.
At first she was so far away her calling was almost
inaudible, then her voice grew in volume and he
thought, she is gone cuckoo again and I don't know
what to do for delirium. And she was back on the
same old track about a horse.

"A horse, Jerry! A horse is right over there—!
Look, look!"

He rose slowly from the depths of his slumber and
opened his eyes to the grey morning. His face was
buried in Heather's hair and he was confused until he
raised his head and realized she was shaking him.

She was still shouting, "The horse. Make him come,
Jerry . . . !"

He reached out to cover her mouth, his dull wits
asking if perhaps this time he would have to seize and
hold her tongue to keep her from choking. Somewhere

he had read or heard about people strangling in delirium.

Then by chance he looked beyond her and was momentarily convinced he was still asleep. For there was a horse moving across a nearby rise in the terrain and there was a man on the horse.

The pilot pushed himself quickly to his feet and waved his arms and yelled incoherently. The horse stopped and he saw the man turn his head. After a moment he took off his wide-brimmed hat and waved it once. He seemed to hesitate a long time before he turned the horse.

The pilot continued his own waving and shouting until the horse was kicking up fountains of snow as it sped toward them.

AT noon Moravia decided to procrastinate one more hour. He was chewing on a peanut-butter sandwich at his desk and noted that his already questionable digestion was not improved by the hands on the wall clock. They were stiff reminders of the sixteen remaining minutes before one o'clock.

When his telephone jingled he picked it up instantly and gave his name. Still chewing he listened, then he stopped chewing as he heard a rancher who identified himself as "Moose" Taylor explain that he was calling at the request of one of Moravia's pilots. He was presently "asleep in my own bed. He is pretty tuckered. I put the little girl on the couch in the front room and I got the Doc on his way. Her back ain't so good but our Doc is."

After Moravia had determined the exact location of the Taylor ranch and asked what he could do immediately he was told, "There ain't nothing you can do right now I guess except maybe give this fella a couple of days off. He said for me to tell you he would like that because there is one letter he wants returned to the sender and he would like to deliver it personally. I dunno what he means by that, but he said it was very important."

"I don't know what it means either," Moravia said. "And I don't care. Just tell him . . . welcome home."